Aunt Millipus and Her Will

Lonnie Graves

EAKIN PRESS ✦ Fort Worth, Texas
www.EakinPress.com

Contents

Chapter 1

The Sign of the Screech Owl

Jason mounted the hill that came to the barbed wire fencerow that separated his father's farmland from that of the pasture. As he opened the wiregap that was used on the gate for wagons, cows, mules, and horses and even himself, he noticed a lazy moon, red-faced round peeping over the eastern horizon and wondered what time it was. He did not have to wonder long, for almost at that moment he heard the crow of a rooster and he immediately recognized it as his mother's big Rhode Island Red. The crow was immediately followed by what he recognized was the little Bantam rooster, who seemed to have a monopoly on the time, for he knew that it was about midnight.

How, he wondered, could a chicken tell what time of night it was, and how could they know in the darkest hour of the night that daylight was approaching. Closing the gap and picking up his shotgun and knapsack, he, together with his two dogs, headed for the house a half-mile away. He was surprised to see a light in the kitchen, for his parents and brothers and sister always went to bed no later than ten o'clock, and since it was now midnight, he wondered what might be going on. They always put the oil lamp out when they went to bed.

He found himself walking faster as he approached the house with the dogs closely beside him as if they were his guards. And indeed they were, for people knew not to mess with

Jason Winfield if his dogs were around, for those coon dogs would tear you to pieces.

As he entered the yard, he could see his mother through the kitchen window. Hurriedly, he went to the back steps and knocked. He heard her voice. "Who knocked?"

He replied, "It's me Momma—Jason."

She quickly unlocked the door and asked, "Boy, where you been this time of night? I couldn't sleep so I decided I'd get up and iron your clothes I washed this morning so I'd have them ready for you when y'all get ready to leave. When is it? Tuesday?"

"Yes ma'am, Momma. Tuesday morning."

Hating to bring up the question of his leaving home, she asked, "Did you kill anything tonight?"

"Not one thing," he replied. "The dogs treed a coon down on the creek, but the branches and leaves were so thick, and it was so dark I could not spot him. I just had to shoot my gun, but I guess I missed him."

"You guess," she replied. "You must have missed him or he would've fell out of the tree on the ground, Jay." They both laughed.

"You are quite right my dear Momma—the one and only Mrs. Lucinda Winfield."

"You," she replied, "and as Professor Love would say, 'Miss Wade Winfield.'"

"Is he asleep? I mean Papa."

"Sleeping like a log," she said, "and I don't think he heard the hounds running that coon, but I did, and I heard the gunshot."

"Listen," she said, "I almost forgot to tell you that Aunt Millipus was over today, and she brought you and me a little bowl of dewberry cobbler, and she told me that this cobbler was for you. She also told me that I could cook my own husband a cobbler if I wanted to since the dewberries were ripe on the fencerow now.

"I said, 'Thank you Aunt Millipus, and I put the cobbler up there in the safe and plain forgot it when we ate supper."

Jason opened the screen mesh door to the safe. He got the bowl, looked in the safe drawer, got a spoon, and attacked the pie hungrily. "Hmm. Boy that sure is good," he said.

"You mean 'sho' was good'. And you had your elbows on the table young Mr. Jay, and I hate to have to remind you again that that is not good table manners."

"I concede, Madam Winfield," he said, standing and bowing, "but I would like to add, with your permission, that it's not 'it sho' was good', but it sure was good or delicious. Thank you professor to me, Mr. Professor Jason."

They both laughed again, and she felt proud. She thought of how much she would miss him when he left. She went to the cook stove carrying a smoothing iron, and with a cloth picked up another iron, turned it over, and spat on it. The spit formed a bubble and rolled off the iron.

"And that's how you tell when it's hot enough huh?"

"Yes," she replied, "that's how I tell. O, yes, and I don't want to forget this, Aunt Millipus said to tell you don't forget that you 'spose to bring 'fessor Love over to her house before you'all leave. She said you be sho' . . . I'm sorry professor . . . sure to come with him for two reasons. One, that folks won't be saying she had the teacher in her house by herself and two, she wanted you to come with him to show her how to make out her will. She wants you to be a witness. Lord, I just wonder who she'll will the acre and a half and that two-room house to. She ain't got no kinfolk, and I believe she got a little money somewhere. She is so distant from most people, but she is a really good-hearted woman."

"I told Aunt Millipus that Professor Love and I would come over Monday night, and he would show her how to make her will. Told her she could carry it to a lawyer at county seat, and he would do the rest," Jason answered.

His mother continued, "she told me that on her way over here she met Uncle Sam Moore, and she said that he asked her where she was going. After finding out that she was going down to Wade's house, he had the nerve to ask her what she had in her bucket. She told him that she had a big bowl of dewberry cobbler and was taking it to the finest young man in this community, Jason Winfield. She said that she was saying that not only because it was true but also because she knew Uncle Sam Mose's baby girl, Violet, was crazy about Jason. She said she knew that Uncle Sam Mose hates 'that boy.' Uncle Sam Mose told her that he knew you were looking at his daughter, but that you . . . he called you a black buzzard . . . would never be a son-in-law of his unless it's over his dead body."

Jason turned the chair around and straddled his legs across the seat. With arms folded on the back he asked, "And what did Aunt Millipus say to that? Knowing her, she had to have the last word."

"Aunt Millie said, 'Cindy, I was mad. I said to him, You old hairy Billy goat . . . you old half-white turkey . . . you old white folks pimp . . . Jason Winfield ain't black, in the first place . . . he is a tall, handsome, brown-skin seventeen-year-old young man and got more sense than all you Moore's put together.'

"Aunt Millie said she told him that she felt sorry for his wife Clara May. Millie said she hoped she lived to throw dirt in his pole face the way he'd treated his wife 'cause his wife wasn't no yellow woman. He knew that when he married her. She said that Jason would have all kinds of girls wanting to marry him. Millie also told him that his sweet little Violet would do well to get in line and forsake the old goat and cleave to Jay, and they could become one. She told him to put that in his pipe and smoke it."

Jason stood up then and patting his hand said, "Hooray, for Aunt Millipus, bravo, bravo, that's telling him."

"Not so loud, son, you'll wake up your papa."

"Yes Momma, but I'm dead serious," he said, "one of these days when I get my education I intend to marry Violet Moore, not because she took color after Uncle Sam, but because she took ways after her momma Aunt Clara. You have to know Violet inside. She's real, momma, and I think I'm in love with her. I believe she loves me even though I'm just seventeen years old and she is sweet sixteen. I have a letter right here in my pocket.'"

He put his hand on the bib pocket of his overalls. "I have a letter in my pocket I received from her today, but don't ask me to let you read it. I'll tell you something she said in it.

"She said, 'Jay, it's going to be hard seeing you leave us. I am going to miss you, but I know you are coming back. I hope not with another girl. Until then I'll be waiting for us to start over."

Lucinda said, "Honey, you know I won't be at the school closing tomorrow night, because my baby will be coming in less than a month. So I want you to say your speech to me. I want to hear it Jay, so just say it to me tonight."

"Oh, Momma—do I haft to?" Jay asked.

"Yes, Jay, I want to hear you say it. I won't be there. I want to hear you say your speech. Do I have to say please?" asked his Momma.

"All right, Momma." He stood up, put his hands beside him, cleared his throat and said, "Four score and seven years ago, our fathers . . . wait Momma, I'm sorry, I've got to start over."

He paused and began again. "The Lincoln Gettysburg Address, by Abraham Lincoln:

Four score and seven years ago, our fathers brought forth to this continent a new nation, conceived in liberty and dedicated to the proposition that all men are created equal. Now we are engaged in a great civil war, testing whether that nation or any nation so . . .

At that moment, from outside the house in a tree came a screeching, shrill sound like a child blowing a whistle. It was without a doubt a screech owl, and Lucinda seemed to freeze in her chair. Jason looked at her. He asked anxiously, "Momma, what's the matter? Are you sick?"

She just sat there a moment reeling and rocking from side to side and saying nothing. He went quickly to her and asked again, "Momma, are you sick? Momma, what's the matter?"

She answered in a whisper, "That's a death owl. It is the sign of death!"

"But Momma . . . ."

"No, son, somebody is going to die. I hate that old owl. He hollered every night down that fencerow up until about a week ago and then he started hollering again. But this is the first time the owl came in my yard out of the tree. It's a sign that somebody in my family is going to die. Lord, help. Lord, please help me."

"But Momma," Jason pleaded, "how can an owl know someone is going to die?"

"Son," she answered, "I don't say the owl knows, but God uses the bird to warn us. He can use anything he makes." At that moment the shrill screech came again, and she reached down, pulled off her left shoe, and placed it bottom upward on the wooden floor.

"And what is that for?" Jason asked.

"To choke him and make him hush," she replied.

Jason picked up his gun and said, "I'll go outside and shoot him."

"No," she said, "you can't see him among the leaves, and I don't want you to wake up Papa and the children."

"Then I'll go out there and chunk a rock into the tree and send him off."

Quickly, he moved to the door, softly opened it, and found a big rock. He threw it powerfully into the tree branches. A flutter was heard, and then he vaguely saw by the brilliant moonlight the bird fly quickly away. Jason went back into the house and said to his mother, "Don't worry anymore. He's gone."

"I'm tired," she said. "I think I'll go to bed. Put the iron on the back of the stove and put the ironing board up. You go to bed. It's late, and you got a busy day tomorrow. Good night, son."

"Good night, Momma," he replied. But from now on he knew there would be no sleep for him, not for a while any way. Why did a screech owl have to spoil the last night with his momma before his graduation? What did the screech owl have to do with somebody dying?

Chapter 2

Thirty Pieces of Silver

Jason put things up like his mother told him, and even though it was late, he decided to take a bath. He went outside and drew two big buckets of water from the well. He filled up the teakettle and a dishpan that was still hot, and while the water heated, he brought in a washtub and sat waiting. He would cool it down with another bucket of water. As he sat there he began to reminisce about events from earlier in the evening. He had been on the woodpile chopping and splitting wood for his mother's cook stove. He had built a rack and had his brothers Henry and Louis stacking firewood in the rack. He wanted to be sure that his mother had an ample supply of wood for a long time and that his father and next oldest brother, who would be helping his papa in the farm work, would not have to worry about cutting up stove wood.

While he was still cutting wood, his father, who had just finished feeding the mules, came out to the woodpile. He sat on top of some logs and said, "Son, I want to talk to you." Jason stopped chopping and faced his father. He stood with both hands on top of the ax handle with the ax between his legs. "Come over and sit down," his father said and Jason obeyed.

"Jay," he said, "you have been a good boy. Never give me no trouble. I am proud of you. That is why I made up my mind that your momma, and me would let you go to the city and get you an education. Now I just went through the third grade in school, and I don't want to hold you back. When 'fessor Love first ask me 'bout you going to college, I told him—no. I needed you to help me on the farm. But he said to me, 'Mr. Winfield, Jason is a smart boy, and you need to let him go to school to make his future better. This is just a seventh grade school, and he'll be finishing this year. He needs to keep on studying. Mr. Winfield, there is a college in the city where I live, and I can get him in. I can get him a job working at the school and in two years, if he studies hard, he can be a teacher.' He said, 'Give him a chance, Mr. Winfield, you won't regret it.' I told him to come over and talk to me and Cindy together, and he did. We decided we wanted you to get your education and we'll take care of the farm.

"Now I got something else I need to tell you," he continued. "I never told you this before, but I want you to know this 'cause if anything ever happens to me, I want you to take care of your momma and sisters and brothers." He looked all around to be sure no one was listening.

"My momma told me," he began, "that I was born four years before President Lincoln freed the slaves in Texas. My papa and momma were slaves of Col. Philip Winfield. Ten acres of land right here where we is sitting. Papa build a log house and grubbed stumps and cut down trees and brushes, bought him a pair of mules, a turning plow, and started making a living on this land. But he did stop working for Colonel Winfield. He helped the colonel and the colonel helped him. Colonel Winfield got hurt in the Civil War and never was real well again. My older brothers left here and went to the territory and never come back. I had to quit school when I was thirteen to keep Papa, and I went to work for Colonel Winfield. Papa and me saved our little money that Colonel Winfield paid us. Papa bought ten more acres of land for $15 an acre. Papa and the colonel died two years apart, when I was seventeen years old. I had to take care of momma and the farm and still work for Ms. Susanna Winfield. Lucinda and me married when I was eighteen and you was born in the one-room log cabin. After we were married, I worked hard and cut cedar trees and built me a big two-room house. Later I built a shed room for Cindy to have a kitchen. Before the colonel died, he and his wife had a grandson who came to live with them. I was surprised and think they was too 'cause he ain't much older than you. I took care of him just like I took care of you. You know . . . Chester . . . I saved him from drowning in the stock tank. I showed him how to ride the horse, and he followed me anywhere. He wanted to stay with us, but Mrs. Winfield wouldn't let him. You know, she did tell me to bring you up to the big house so you could stay with Chester. When Mrs. Winfield found out that this farm was for sale, she bought the land and sold it to me because the people would not have let me buy it."

His father looked real serious and he repeated, "This is something I want you to know. You remember when Cindy and me ordered this stuff from the mail order store? Remember the day that me and you went to Koohne Town in the wagon to pick up the stuff at the railroad station?"

Jason never forgot that day. He remembered well when his father loaded the barrel from the train onto his wagon. He also remembered what Clyde and Claude Black had asked him. "Where did you get money to order all of that stuff? You been stealing something from Ms. Winfield? I know you didn't make enough money off twenty acres of land to buy all that stuff 'specially that new buggy you got. So you must of been stealing."

The railroad station owner had said to Clyde and Claude, "Y'all best let Wade alone. Ms. Winfield trusts Wade 'cause he takes care of her stuff, and if you bother with him you'll be in trouble with Ms. Winfield. You know she's one of the most powerful women in this community."

They had tried to laugh it off as Jason was steaming inside. He wondered why his papa didn't talk back to these two white men, because his papa was a brave man who would fight anybody. He was strong. Jason had seen him throw a big yearling down by himself. He'd have Jason hold the head while holding the feet for someone to castrate the yearling.

So as they rode off, Jason kept twisting his hands together and his father knew that he was angry. After a while, as they rode alone back home, his papa said, "Son, I need to tell you something else. Don't ever think all white folks is bad. There is good white folks, and there is bad white folks. Just like there is good colored folks and bad colored folks. And Clyde and Claude is bad white folks. Bad folks come to no good end. Now you take old man Richard Koohne, he is a good white man, and he's got plenty of money. He owns the bank. He owns Koohne Lumber Company, Koohne Grocery Store, and thousands of acres of land. But he helps colored people. He's a good man. Now you take Mrs. Winfield. She is a good white woman. All I'm saying son is that there are good folks in all races, and I ain't scared of Claude and I ain't scared of Clyde. But some things you have to turn over to the Lord."

Jason listened as his father continued. "I want to tell you about Uncle Bud Wright . . . you remember him. He came up the road one evening from toward the river with a sack on his shoulder. I had never seen him before. He looked tired and asked us for some water. Cindy got the bucket and the dipper and gave him some water. And then he told us he was from Alabama and was looking for a place to stay. He said, 'I'm an old man, but I can chop and grub and fix fences and if I find a place to stay, I'll work for nothing but food and a place to sleep.'

"So me and Cindy decided to let him live in Papa and Momma's old log cabin. The bed, benches, and old cook stove was all still there. Cindy kept it clean and locked up, so we took Uncle Bud in and when Cindy cooked she fed Uncle Bud just like she did y'all.

"Cindy loved Uncle Bud 'cause he helped her in her garden. He milked the cow for her and he watched after y'all, and she just loved him. And he learned to love her. Uncle Bud liked to fish. So we bought him fishing lines and hooks, and he'd dig worm bait and go to the river on his spare time and fish. Well, he stayed there in Papa's house 'bout two years and was just like one of the family. Then you remember this . . . one day he just left. He didn't tell me or Cindy or anybody. He just left."

Jason's mind began to click as he remembered the day that Uncle Bud left. Uncle Bud had called him and given him a little sack and said to him, "Keep this 'til in the morning. Don't open it. Just keep it and give it to your momma and papa." And he was gone.

The next morning, Jay did what Uncle Bud had told him to do. Jason said to his parents, "Uncle Bud told me to give y'all this." His momma and papa unwrapped the sack. In the sack was a twenty-dollar gold piece wrapped in a ball of cotton. They were shocked and asked, "Jason, where did Uncle Bud get a twenty dollar gold piece? Where did he go? Why didn't he tell anybody? Jason, Did he tell you where he was going?"

"No sir, no ma'am. All he said was to give y'all the sack." He remembered how they had kept the money for a while and then when they never heard from him, they had spent the money.

Jason remembered the water in the teakettle and the dishpan and he walked over to test the temperature. When he sat back down in his chair, his father said, "Two years later, you remember, one Saturday evening Uncle Bud walked back in this yard. He was sick, walking on a stick, and we were overjoyed to see him. We asked him where he'd been. He said, "Y'all just let me rest, I'm sick.'"

His father continued to tell the story. "Me and Cindy unlocked the old house and carried him in. Cindy fixed the bed and let him lay down. She fixed him some food, but we could tell he was sick. No matter how Cindy doctored on him and fed him, he didn't seem to get no better. His leg swoll up, his stomach swoll up, and he would have to sit up in the chair to sleep. He couldn't stay by himself no longer. We brought him over here in our house where we could watch him day and night. We did everything we knowed to do for him, but he just got worse.

Then, one night in November he called me and Cindy and said, 'I want to tell y'all something—why I left and where I went and why I came back. I always intended to come back.' I remember how he lowered his voice, took a breath and said, 'One day, I went fishing on the bayou and while I was fishing I walked up the stream a little piece. I seen this big tree that had almost caved in the bayou from that last big rain that we had. Sticking out from under the roots I seen this crock jar. I went to see what it was and I took a stick and dug around that crock till I could get it out. When I got it out, I set it down on the ground, took the top off, and in it was twenty-five twenty-dollar gold pieces.'

"Uncle Bud said he was scared but he continued telling us the story. He said, 'I didn't know whether that tree was on your property or somebody else's property. I didn't know where the line was, and I know you are a honest man. If I had told you, you would have more likely made me give the money back to the people who owned the property. So I climbed the bank, went in the bushes, and counted the money. There were twenty-five twenty-dollar gold pieces. Under it were thirty pieces of silver. Thirty pieces of silver dollar. So, since I didn't know what to do, I hid the money in the bushes till late that evening when I went back where the money was with a grubbing hoe and a shovel and one of your iron wagon rods. I went to a big live oak tree

11

and made an 'x' with my knife on the south side, about head high, and I walked south for forty steps and I drove a stab down. I then walked west for forty steps to a little ditch. Right on the other side of the ditch was a little pecan tree.

"Uncle Bud said, 'It was night now. I took six of those gold pieces out and put them in my pocket. I took that hoe and shovel and buried the rest of that money in that pot in that ditch. I took the iron wagon rod and drove it all the way down and covered it up with some old bushes. That's when I left. I wanted to go to Alabama and see my sick brother. So I gave Jay one gold piece to give y'all. I caught the train and paid my fare with money that y'all had been giving me to get to the city. When I got to the city, I used some of the gold to buy me a ticket to Alabama. I stayed with my brother until he died, and then I said I'm going back to Texas.'

"Uncle Bud said, 'Here I am. Now y'all know what happened to me. I want you and Cindy to have that money. Find that tree with an "x" on it. Go south and you will see a post in the ground—forty steps to the ditch and you will find a wagon rod and money is in that ditch. Now I'm gonna die. I'm sick, and Wade I want you to buy Lucinda a brand new buggy with rubber tires and a top on it so she can ride nice like some of the other women.'

'Now I want you to promise me. Wade, I want you to give the thirty pieces of silver to Rev. Prince for the church. Take the rest of the money for you and the children.'

"And then he said, 'Now, let me down in the bed.'

Father said, "Your momma was crying. She went and got a cold, wet rag and washed his face. You remember, I woke you up and told you to get Uncle Frank Cotton. Cindy told you to get Aunt Millipus.

"That night Uncle Bud died. Your momma took it hard." Father remembered how he sent for Rev. Prince, who lived about eight miles away, and they buried Uncle Bud that evening in Ever Green Cemetery. "Jay, I know you remember this," Father continued. "After the burying, me and your momma talked about what he told us about the money."

"We wondered was Uncle Bud really telling us the truth or was he so sick he was out of his mind. Your momma said, 'But what about the twenty dollar gold piece he gave us?' We didn't know. There are lot of oak trees in that pasture. So, where do you start to look for an oak tree with a "x" made on it? I just really didn't believe Uncle Bud's story."

12

Father said, "So we talked about it and one day Cindy said, 'You know Wade, Uncle Bud, was a truthful man, I don't think he was telling no story. I think you need to try to find that tree.' So, one evening I went down in the pasture and looked at oak trees until it was getting late. I was about to give up when I saw this big oak tree with an "x" on the south side. It was about head high like he said. And like he told me, I walked forty steps south—back toward this house—and walked upon an oak stick still in the ground. I took forty steps west and sure 'nuff there was a shallow ditch and right across the ditch was a pecan tree, just like Uncle Bud said. Now I wasn't scared, I took my ax and dug in the ground, loosed the ground until I hit something. I took my hands and uncovered it and there was the wagon rod. I was excited. I went back to the house and told Cindy what I found.

"So, that night, me and your momma took the lantern and the shovel and the shotgun. We told y'all that me and her was going to walk down the road and look for some rabbits and for y'all to stay home until we got back. We went back to that ditch, and I pulled the rod out of the ground and took my shovel and started digging. Me and Cindy both were scared 'cause we always heard if somebody gives you some money, you can't talk. I began to dig. Seems like I could hear things and Cindy was holding on to me while I was digging, and I told her to put the lantern down in the ditch so nobody could see the light. The deeper I dug, it seemed like I could hear noises. I kept digging until I hit something with the shovel. When I dug it out, it was a rock. I pulled the rock out and felt down there. I felt that crock. I dug it out and opened it, took the top off and just like Uncle Bud said, and in that jar was gold money. I covered the ditch up, and we come back to the house with the money. We counted it. Uncle Bud had nineteen twenty-dollar gold pieces and thirty silver dollars.

"When I got to the house, I hid the money. Cindy didn't want me to leave it in the house, so I had to hide it outside. I'm giving you one of those twenty-dollar gold pieces. With the money you saved selling hides and so forth, this will get you by for a while. Before you go to school in the city I'm going to tell you where I hid it. But before I hid the money, I took some of the money and went to the city and bought Lucinda a rubber-tire buggy with a top on it.

"I remember how happy everyone was when I came home

with the new buggy. How excited. I remember how she hitched the horse to it and rode to visit people in the community and all the way up to Red Bluff."

And then Jason remembered when his father opened the barrel and all of those things were in there. There were also some things in there that Miss Millipus had ordered. There were also some things for other people who had all put it in their order. So it really wasn't all just the family. There were neighbors who had put in their order also. Before Momma sent off the order she took the tape and measured all their sizes—their arms and their feet—to make sure she had the right sizes for their coats and things. He remembered how they opened the box and tried on their clothes, and how nearly they were to fitting them perfectly, and how happy they were at that time.

His father went on talking and said, "I did have some money left, Jay, so I'm giving you twenty dollars this evening. I do have more left. I hid it, and Cindy doesn't even want me to tell her where it is. She's just kind of funny like that. I want to tell you so if anything ever happens to me and you come home, you'll know where this other money is. I saved the money so you can have a little bit, and I'm giving you twenty dollars so you can have some extra money. I kept some of the money and I got it hid. To tell you the truth, I got ten twenty-dollar gold pieces left. I hid it here on the place . . . ."

By that time he lowered his voice and said, "Oh, here comes Uncle Frank, I'd better hush."

Uncle Frank rode up on his horse and said, "Hey, Wade what's going on?"

"Nothin', we just talking."

"Y'all talking 'bout something I don't need to hear?"

"Naw, man, get off your horse and come on in."

Father said, "Jason, go on, I'll talk with you later . . . I got something for you before I go." Then he paused. He continued by talking to Uncle Frank. "You know Jason is finishing school."

"Oh yeah I know about that." Uncle Frank said.

Father said, "He will be going off to school with Professor Love, so I bought him a present that I want him to have." Father went in the barn and dug in the corn and came back and gave the present to Jason. It was a shotgun. Jason was so happy with his present. His father also gave him the shells to the gun. He remembered his father saying to him, "We'll finish our conversation later, Jay, is that all right?"

Jay said, "Yes sir, Papa, yes sir."

Uncle Frank said, "Well, if y'all were talking about something . . . ."

Father said, "Naw that was O.K. we were just talking about him and his work and we're finished now . . . come on up on the porch and sit down. Tie your horse down—come on." Jay remembered that his father didn't get to tell him at that time where the money was.

After he poured the water in the tub and cooled it with another bucket of water, he took his bath and later lay down on a soft cotton mattress, which he was so thankful for. He remembered when he was a young boy that they had some shuck mattresses and now he had a nice soft mattress, which he and his brother Henry Lee shared. He lay there and finally went to sleep.

The next morning, Jason slept later than usual. His parents did not disturb him but just let him sleep. It was a beautiful day. Late April; the sun was shining brightly, and the wind was blowing. His mother was already cooking dinner for him to carry to his school-closing affair. He walked into the kitchen and said, "Good morning, Momma."

She replied, "Good morning, my son. What time did you finally get to bed?"

He replied, "It was pretty late." She asked if he felt all right and he assured her that he did. She told him to come and get some breakfast and that she was cooking dinner all at the same time too.

She told him to go outside and call his father and tell him to come and eat his breakfast. The family always ate together. As they sat down to eat, he was thankful that they now had chairs with backs to them instead of benches he remembered that they had earlier. When they finished breakfast, his father went back out to see about the cows. Jay gathered his things, got his ball and glove and bat, and took off to school.

This was a great day in Sandy Lane School. It was known as Exhibition Day. Mrs. Love, Professor Love's wife, had taught the girls how to crochet and embroider, and they had bought domestic cloth and made bed sheets and pillowcases and embroidered peacocks and things like that on the sheets and pillow cases. They also made scarves for the dressers and washstands and starched them with flour and ironed them for the exhibition. Some of the older girls made dresses with pleats in them. All of this they hung on the walls of the school so that the people would see what they had done beside reading and writing. Professor Love taught the boys how to make a workbench and a bookcase. They were very proud to show these items to their parents.

The feature attraction of the day was a baseball game between the boys from Red Bluff and Sandy Lane schools. The game was to begin after dinner. Jason and his friends were out on the field for practice, and although he was the number one pitcher, he chose to go out in the field and play catch while other boys knocked the ball to him.

People had begun to gather around noon at the school with their baskets and tubs from which they would be serving food. One of the boys hit a ball almost to the fence, and although Jason had to run a long way he managed to catch it and throw it all the way in to home plate. When he looked around he saw Aunt Millipus coming across the field in a trail that she had made from her house to the church and school. This trail kept her from going all the way around the road. In one hand she had a basket of food and in the other a tin bucket. When Jason saw her, he jumped the barbed wire fence and went to meet her. He said, "Aunt Millipus, let me carry your things."

She said, "Jason, this basket of food is going to be served to the people but in that bucket are teacakes and they are for you. I ain't serving them." She smiled a little bit and said, "Now, if you want to give Violet some, it's all right. I know you like her and she's a sweet girl. I don't know where she got it. She sho' didn't get it from her pappy and you are a good boy. If you and Violet love each other don't you let ole' man Sam Moore, that old gray haired goat, keep y'all apart."

"Yes ma'am, Aunt Millie," Jason said. They got to the fence and Jason put his foot on one of the lower wires and with his right hand raised the higher wire. Aunt Millie stooped and went through the fence. Jason sat the basket down on the other side of the fence and stepped back a few feet and jumped the fence.

Aunt Millie said, "Boy, you gonna break your neck one day jumping over things with those long legs." Before they got to the school she stopped and asked, "Did you tell Professor Love what I said? You know I told you I want to make out my will and I don't know nothin' about how to do it. I want you and him to come over here before you go to the city. You come with him Jason, you hear me?"

"Yes ma'am." Jason said he could come over Tuesday because he was to leave on Wednesday.

She said, "That'd be good. I'm going to fix you and Professor Love some supper."

A little while later they looked up the road and saw dust flying. It was the folks from Red Bluff School. Some were in wagons, some in buggies, some on horseback, and many of the boys were walking the five miles they had to come. Professor Love and some of the boys went out to welcome them.

Before they served dinner, Sandy Lane School had one more event that stirred up a lot of interest. The little girls were going to wrap the maypole. The maypole was a high pole, which extended about ten feet out of the ground and had ribbons of different colors attached to the top of it. Twelve little girls dressed in paper dresses, which had been made by Mrs. Love, were holding a ribbon, which matched their individual dresses. They held their ribbons out from the pole in a tent-like position. Six of them were to go one way and the other six were to go in the opposite direction around the pole. Each girl criss-crossed each other precisely so that the ribbons would wrap the pole from top to bottom until the pole was wrapped. The girls did it perfectly. Then Mrs. Love had them form a line facing the people and bow. The mothers, sisters, and aunts were so happy. They cheered and cheered and then they served dinner. They had brought such a variety of food for dinner. There were hams, possum and potatoes, chicken and dumplings, fresh turnip greens, and potato pon to name a few.

Now it was time for the ball game. The rivalry between the schools could be compared to that of the New York Yankees and the Brooklyn Dodgers in a world series. Mrs. Love along with Professor Love had taught the children yells to cheer the boys on. She had chosen Violet, one of the Cotton girls, and one of Jay's sisters to be cheerleaders. She had made them white, sailor-style midi blouses and blue skirts, and when they were all in position they started on their first yell. All three of the girls called loudly, "Are you ready?" The rest of the children would reply, "Yes." Then they would say, "What's the matter with Sandy Lane?" And the students would answer, "She's all right." They said, "Who said so?" The answer, "Everybody." The question, "Who is everybody?" The answer, "Sandy Lane." And they all gave a great big yell while clapping their hands. Then they said, "Are you ready?" The answer, "Yes." They said, "One, two three, GO." And they all said together,

When you're up you're up.
And when you're down you're down.
But when you're upside Sandy Lane
Then you're upside down.

At that moment they had a boy dressed in blue pants and a white shirt turn a flip and stand on his hands. Oh, did the crowd get a kick out of that.

It seems that everybody in the community was there with two exceptions for sure—Lucinda, who was eight months pregnant, and Aunt Clara Moore who hardly went to anything. Uncle Sam was there. Uncle Frank Cotton and Aunt Josie were there. She was, as usual, chewing on a toothpick, which she had made from a stem on a tree. Deacon Moses Randolph and Miss Lizzy (she preferred Miss Lizzy instead of Aunt Lizzy because she said she was still a young woman) were also there but had come late because Uncle Moses had to close the store before he could come. Although their house was only a small way from the playground, Mrs. Randolph had him hitch up the horses to their surrey so she could sit up in the surrey and not have to stand and watch the ball game. She had on her broad hat with a hatpin sticking through her hair. She sat gracefully in her surrey and talked to people on the ground. She did finally invite Aunt Josie Cotton to come and sit with her.

The game was scheduled for seven innings. At the bottom of the seven innings the score was tied five to five. Sandy Lane was batting with one out, and Jay was the batter. He had two strikes and on the next pitch he hit the ball, and it seemed that he hit the ball a half a mile. It went out of the clearing and into the weed patch beyond. While he circled the bases the fielders were looking in the weeds to find the ball. Jay had made a home run. Naturally, Sandy Lane went wild. The wife of the principal of Red Bluff cried.

People went home to dress for the school-closing program that night. Jay had put on his new suit and shoes as well as did the other children. Mose, Jay's best friend, had gone home, dressed, and walked down to Jay's house so that they could walk to the church where they were having the program. Violet, who was Mose's first cousin, told him to tell Jay that she wanted to talk to Jay before he left. So they walked together to the church and Violet and one of Jay's sisters was waiting for Jay at the fence. The church was located several hundred feet away from the fence that surrounded it. Violet had on a pink violet dress with a white ribbon running through loops and had a big bow in the back. Her hair hung in two plaits down her back and she had tied pink bows on the end of each plait. She had on baby-doll slippers and pink socks.

Jason said to her, "Violet, you look very pretty. You are always pretty. But tonight you are pretty, pretty."

She blushed and said, "Thank you, Jay." She said, "You look like a prince in your new suit. I'm going to miss you. I hope that you don't fall in love with one of those pretty city girls, because I'll be waiting for you when you come home."

He said, "Violet, I've told you before, and I'm telling you again, I love you and when I come home I want you to be my wife. We will live together always."

"Jay, are you asking me to marry you?"

"Yes I am," he said. "Do I have to get down on my knees?"

"No, you can't mess up your suit."

"Then what is your answer?" he asked.

"My answer is yes, Jay. We will have our lives together."

Mose and his sister were standing a way apart. "You better come on now. Here comes somebody," Mose said to Violet and Jay. Jay held Violet's hand for a moment. He kissed her on the cheek and said again, "I love you."

The school-closing program was great. They held it at the Baptist church because it was larger than the Methodist church. The Baptist church was also closer to the school. The little children said their speeches and sang their songs. In the second part of the program they had a dialogue. Mose was the principal character. Jim Cotton, who played ole' man Scott, was supposed to have three daughters. The Scott's had a party and invited some more girls who were to spend the night. Only girls were invited. However, Harry, who was played by Mose, wanted to go because he liked one of the Scott girls. He had to dress up like a girl to get into the party. Mose's idea was to get some of his sister's things to look like a girl. He found a wig and had to find a very long dress to cover his feet since he couldn't find girl shoes to fit them. Ole' man Scott didn't know that Harry, who was dressed as a girl, was a boy. Mose had a problem talking like a girl, which made ole' man Scott suspicious. He asked Mose questions about where 'she' lived and who her parents were. Finally, when they served their food, Mose dropped a piece of chicken on the floor and when he stooped down to pick it up his wig came off. Ole' man Scott's suspicion was satisfied. He went to get his gun to shoot Mose. Mose ran, crawled, and knocked over things to get out of there. The audience was near tears from laughing at the scene. Mose did get away.

Then came the time for graduation. Mrs. Love played the wind organ in the church, and one of the boys that lived in the bottom had a good voice and sang one of the old folk songs. The words spoke of something about his old Kentucky home. Some of the people who had come from Kentucky as slaves remembered their old home and cried as he sang to the accompaniment played by Mrs. Geraldine Love. Then came the time for the address by the valedictorian. This was the student who had made the highest marks in the class. He said, "Ladies and Gentlemen, I present to you, young Mr. Jason Winfield."

Jason started his address with words from Lincoln's Gettysberg Address. He was interrupted several times by applause. He closed his speech by saying, "the government of the people, for the people and by the people shall not perish from this earth." The audience gave him a standing ovation.

Professor Love presented the diplomas and then asked Deacon Mose Randolph to make some remarks. He mounted the rostrum, and just as he began to speak there was a noise at the front door of the church. In came three men wearing white hoods and carrying shotguns. One of them said, "Don't nobody move and you won't get hurt. All we want is Wade Winfield. He's been rustling cows and selling them and we came to get him. Ain't no way he can buy all these new clothes, wear a new suit, and buy a new buggy just by selling those hides. He ain't made no crop yet so he's been stealing and we aim to break it up."

Wade was sitting by a window. With guns drawn the three men called for Wade to come forth. The audience seemed to be frozen in their seats. Deacon Randolph, still standing on the podium, said, "I don't know who you fellows is, but y'all looking for the wrong man. I know Wade Winfield, and he ain't stole no cows and furthermore this is God's house. Y'all need to git out of here. Whoever you is."

They said, "Shut up ole' man. Wade, come out of there right now."

There were kerosene lamps hanging on the walls with a metal shield between the lamp globe and the wooden wall. Somebody blew the lamp out where Wade was sitting and said,

"Jump out the window, Wade, jump out the window." Someone dared to stand up where Wade was sitting to shield him from the men. People kept shouting, "Jump out the window." Wade jumped out of the window and he heard shouts, "Run to the woods, run to the woods." There was a wooded area about forty feet behind the church, and as Wade ran it was discovered that there were more hooded men outside on horses. These men spotted Wade and shouted, "There he goes through the woods." It was complete bedlam in the church. Women and children were crying, and mothers were trying to gather their families together.

Suddenly, they heard shots in the woods. Then the sound of horse hoofs riding away was heard. Jason ran out of the church, ran into the woods yelling, "Papa, Papa, Papa." Some of the men were running behind him, and Mose came along too. They found Wade lying in a pool of blood. Jason fell on his knees crying, "Papa, Papa." Wade was breathing hard. Jason was trying to lift him up.

Wade said, "Don't lift me up. Jay, take care of your momma and the children."

"Papa," Jay said as he cried.

"Jay, I want you to be a good boy . . . take care of your momma, your sister, and brothers." Then he died.

Uncle Frank Cotton came where Jason was. He kneeled and put his arms around him and said, "Come on, Jason, your father is dead." Other men gathered around. Someone went and got the wagon and put Wade's body in the wagon and carried it home. Aunt Millipus, Aunt Josie Cotton, and two other women went to the house to tell Lucinda what had happened. Mose was right there by Jason's side while someone else went to Koohne's Town to report what had happened. It was a night that they would never forget. The children were still crying. Lucinda sat in her rocking chair with her arms folded. She rocked to and fro and was just groaning.

The men washed the body and laid it on a cooling board. Some of the men and women sat up all night with the body. Early the next morning, Jason went into the room where his mother was lying down. He told her that he was going to take the money he had been saving to go to school and the money that his father gave him and the few dollars that Aunt Millipus and others had given him for his graduation present and he was going to Koohne Town and purchase a casket and pine box to bury his father in. He and Uncle Frank Cotton went to the white undertakers in Koohne Town to get these things, while the men of the community dug the grave on a damp, misty, rainy morning so that they could bury him that afternoon. Parson Prince, pastor of the Baptist church, had suggested to Jason and his mother that because of the weather and because the roads were so muddy from last night's terrible rain that they would not have the funeral that day. Too many of the friends that lived in the bottoms and other places would not be able to attend because of the muddy roads. Since Wade was a faithful deacon in the church, the parson wanted to have a funeral that would compliment his loyalty to the church. They postponed the funeral until the first of July. This way Lucinda's baby would have been born and she would be able to attend the funeral.

Jason was quiet practically all the way to Koohne Town, and Uncle Frank left him alone. After they started back, however, Uncle Frank said, "Jay, I need to tell you something. Something like this happened in my family when I was a boy. A mob crowd killed my brother. So, I don't want you to think that you can take this into your own hands and try to get the people who are responsible for your papa's death. That is what the law is for. I know how you must feel, but Uncle Frank is going to tell you what is best for you. You can't fight these white folks by yourself. Your papa was a good man and a honest man. He was a Christian man."

Jason said, "And my papa ain't stole no cows. That just ain't true, Uncle Frank. My papa ain't stole no cows."

Uncle Frank said, "I know your papa ain't stole no cows Jason, but you let the law and God handle this thing. Uncle Frank ain't gonna tell you nothing but what's right. I am not going to ask you to promise this to me right now because I know how you feel inside. But Jay, think about what I have said to you today. Promise me that."

"I promise, Uncle Frank," Jason said.

They got back to the cemetery and took the box out and made sure that the grave was long and wide enough for it. The grave was six feet deep. They went on to the house, took the casket out, carried it inside, and laid the dressed body in the casket. Lucinda was brought into the room to view the body. She stood there, saying over and over, "Bye Wade. Bye Wade." It was a very emotional time for the entire family.

The rain was still falling lightly as though it was grieving with the community. They carried Wade to the cemetery, lowered him into the pine box, which was already in the grave, and Parson Prince picked up a handful of dirt and committed the body to the ground, saying "Earth to earth, ashes to ashes, and dust to dust." The men picked up their shovels and covered the grave. Parson Prince dismissed those people who had braved the rain to be at the burial. Aunt Millipus was there. Instead of her going home, she went straight to the woods where Wade had been killed. Jason watched her and saw her kneeling down as though she was looking for something, and he wondered what she was doing. Then, as if it were a tribute to the family, the sun suddenly came out as Mose walked with Jason back to the house.

On Sunday morning Mrs. Winfield came in on the train from the east where she had been visiting her grandson in college. When she got the news that Wade was dead, she was very upset, and on her arrival home she immediately had her cook prepare food for Lucinda and her family. She even took linens for beds and loaded all those things in her surrey. One of her hired men drove her to Wade's house. When they arrived, she stepped briskly out of the surrey and onto the porch calling out, "Lucinda, Lucinda. This is Mrs. Winfield." Some of the neighbors who were there, said, "Come in Mrs. Winfield." She said, "Lucinda, I am hurt. I am mad. I don't like this and we are going to find out who did it. I'm mad Lucinda. Wade never stole anything from me all these years. I could trust him with anything I had. He saved my grandson's life when he went swimming in a tank down there. Somebody lied on Wade, and I'm going to get a lawyer so we can find out who did this."

Mrs. Winfield looked around the room with an element of surprise, for she had never been in Wade's house before. The iron bed was made up and a white counterpane (bedspread) with tassels on the side was very neatly made up. A dresser was beside the bed with a tall mirror in it. Near the fireplace was a washstand with a large white bowl and a large white pitcher in the bowl. A linen towel hung on the rack. This was used on special occasions. A store-bought rug was on the floor. It was made of cloth and woven straw. There were curtains at the windows.

Mrs. Winfield said, "Lucinda, this is nice. This is nice. I brought you some things. Now I want to see the rest of the house." When she had gone through the house, she came back and gave Lucinda some money. She said, "I'm going now. Anything you need you send Jay up there and I'll give it to him. Whenever he can work for me, come right on." Then she turned to the children and said, "You children, mind your momma." Jay walked with her to the surrey and helped her back in. She said to him. "Take care of your momma. Don't y'all suffer for nothing. You come up there whenever you get ready. We're going to see to it that whoever did this will have to pay."

Professor Love decided to stay on for another week. This had changed everything. He felt he owed it to Jay to stay and help him take a new road in his life. Jay said, "Professor Love, I want to thank you for all you have done for us. I guess it wasn't to be for me to go to school, but I have to take care of Momma and my sisters and brothers.

Professor Love said, "Jay, I want you to know this. Sometimes the road to the top is by stepping-stones and a quitter never wins. A winner never quits till he gets to the top. So do what you have to do. Perhaps these are stones that will take you higher because, Jay, you have what it takes to be a man. I see it in you. Mark my words, I may never live to see it, but one day you will be Mr. Jason Winfield. As I promised you, I am going to stay until we talk to Aunt Millipus about her will. So maybe Friday, you and I will go down to her house and hear what's she got to tell us. Can you do that late Friday evening? She thinks a lot of you."

"Yes, Professor Love. I am anxious to hear her story," Jason said. "I won't forget what you have told me today. I won't forget. I promise you."

Chapter 3

Aunt Millipus

A little before sundown on Friday evening, Jay and Professor Love walked up the road together to Aunt Millipus' house. Her house was about a mile away. She was sitting on her porch and invited them in and told them she had fixed them a little meal. They went through the bedroom and into her kitchen where she had set a table with her nice dishes, forks, spoons, knives, tablecloth, napkins, and glasses. She even had candles lit. She knew how to set a table because all of her life she had worked for people who had these kind of things. She even had picked roses from her yard and had them in a vase on the table. She served them a tasty meal. She had both coffee and lemonade. When they had finished, she took them back into her bedroom where there were two rocking chairs, a straight chair, and another piece of furniture. This was a large room with a fireplace. A small trunk sat in one of the corners of her room, and a lamp set on the center of the table. The table was traditionally called the center table.

They both, without saying, were startled at Aunt Millipus' attire. When Aunt Millipus pulled off her apron, underneath she had on a long, flowing dress that was a light blue color. Her hair was not wrapped nor was it plaited. It was combed and hung down her back. She had on no head rag, no kind of head covering. She had some expensive looking earrings, and it surprised them because they had never seen anything but straws in her pierced ears. The mole on her face accentuated her unusual appearance. Professor Love whispered to Jay, "I never saw her look like this."

Aunt Millipus sensed what they had whispered. She reached with her hands and rolled her hair into a ball on the top of her head. She stuck a large hairpin in it to keep it from coming apart. They realized that Aunt Millipus was not an old woman. She couldn't have been over fifty years old.

She stood there before the fireplace and prepared herself for the story she was going to tell them. She thanked them both for coming. "I want to warn both of you," she said, "that this is a long story. So if you don't think you can put up with my story, you have a chance to back out right now."

Professor Love said, "Aunt Millipus, we want to hear your story. Take your time. If you have the time, we have the time."

She went to her rocker, sat down, and said, "This is it. My momma told me I was born a slave in Alabama. She named me Emily. Everyone called me Millie. She said that her slave owner gave her boys to his daughter for a wedding present when she married some man in South Carolina. She never saw them again. She told me that my father was a white man. I never knew him. We were the slaves of a man named Stone and so my name was Millie Stone. When I was a little girl, ole man Stone died. They put some of his slaves on the slave block in Montgomery, Alabama. A man by the name of Col. George Jackson bought me; my momma and a young slave man by the name of Aaron Stone carried us to Mississippi to his plantation that was called Jackson Quarters. Momma was a good cook and housekeeper. This is what she did in the big house. I was a little young girl, and he and his wife had one child. The child was a boy who was about six years older than I was. His name was George Jr. Mrs. Jackson and George taught me how to read and write and set tables. My momma and me stayed in a little house in the back of the big house.

"When I was about fifteen years old, Colonel George gave me to his son Master George for his mistress. Neither my momma nor I had any choice in the matter. He moved momma upstairs in the back of the house. This was a great big house. He let me stay in the servant house where William could sleep with me whenever he wanted to. I cannot say that I loved William.

26

He was nice to me. He called me his little yellow hammer because of my color. There was also a bird called yellow hammer. I still helped in the house and when I was about sixteen years old, I had a son by Master George Jr. About a year and a half later I had a daughter. I named the boy Johnie and the girl Jennie Mae. They both were white children and I loved my children. Ole man Colonel George and Master George Jr. bought them clothes, shoes, and saw that they were well taken care of.

"About that time Mrs. Jackson died leaving Colonel George and Master George Jr. in that big house. Like I said, I liked Master George Jr. but I could not say that I was in love with him. I often wondered what it would be like to be with one of the black boys down in the quarters. But that was not to be 'cause Mr. George was very sensitive about whoever talked to me—especially if it was a man. Then one night, Mr. George told me he was going to get married, and I said, 'So, this ends our sleeping together.' He said, 'No.' I said, 'What do you mean—No. Do you think that your wife would want to put up with that kind of situation? And what about my feelings?' And he said to me, 'She would marry me under any condition. She knows about you and these children. She wants to get in this house because her folks are poor folks. I told her about you and nothing will be changed. You will still be my little yellow hammer because these are my children.'

"He married her. I know y'all looking at me funny. That's how it was. He slept with his wife and slept with me. I cooked because Momma was having rheumatism and I also kept the house.

"I didn't particularly like Mr. George's wife. She was a pretty redheaded girl. But she was wild. She liked to have parties and there were always men around the house. To me she didn't seem to love Mr. George that much. But she loved where she was living.

"One day—I guess my boy was about five years old—they called all of the slaves together and told us that we had been set free. We were free to go where we wanted to go and live where we wanted to live. But Col. George Jackson told the slaves that if they wanted to work for him, he would let them work the crops with his mules and give them half of whatever they made. Many of them stayed.

"I said, 'Mr. George, don't look at me so hard y'all.' Mr. George said, 'I can't let you go my little yellow hammer. You stay here. I'll pay you wages to work in the house. You got a house to stay in and Papa and me will feed you out of the big house. You won't have to buy no groceries. I will constantly remind you that these are my children and I'm going to take care of them.'

"Then his wife had a baby. I stayed on. I know that this might sound crazy but I had no place to go. My momma had died and I had two little white children. So, I nursed Mr. George and his wife's little boy. But there was something wrong with the little boy. He had spells and he would fall out in the floor at times and foam at the mouth. You would think he was going to die. After that he would be all right for a time.

"After Col. George Jackson died, Mr. George took over the plantation. About this time all of the farm people started calling Mr. George, Col. George. I even did it. One day a stranger named Harvey, a young black man, came there looking for a job. He was six feet tall, I suppose, brown skin, neat young man. He could rope, ride, and break horses. He was just a very good farm hand. To me he was just a good-looking colored man. Colonel George hired him to feed the horses and the mules and see about the cows. He didn't work in the fields. I would see him everyday. He always walked with pride. I admired him greatly. I suppose he must have been about twenty-six or twenty-seven years old.

"One day, I was out under the peach tree picking some peaches and a wasp stung me. I did not see the wasp nest and they were swarming. I cried out, and he ran and grabbed me from that swarm of wasps. He pulled me into the smokehouse. He shut the door until the wasps went away. He put some tobacco juice on my sting, and there in that smokehouse for the first time I knew I was in love. He asked me if I was all right and I said yes. I said thank you and then for a moment he took me in his arms. I had never had a feeling like this for a man before in my life. I immediately left him and went back to my house. I knew if Colonel George found this out he would send that man away, and I felt like I had to know this man better.

"Sure enough, as it was, we became lovers. When this happened, I dreaded the colonel coming to my room. If when I was younger I had responded to his love, I didn't want to anymore. I wanted to save my love for this man whose name was Harvey. When George came to my room at night, I would pretend to be sick because I wanted excuses for him to leave me alone. One night, he asked me why I was acting so strangely. I said, 'Well, you have wife colonel.' He said, 'I told you, you don't have to call me colonel while we are together.' I told him I was grieving over my mother, but it wasn't that. He would leave me and go to the big house.

"Harvey would come out of the quarters. I would have a lamp in my window and my signal to come would be for me to put the lamp out. Harvey would come and stay with me until three or four o'clock in the morning. Harvey said to me, 'One of these days, Millie, I want to take you away from here. There are places like Memphis, Atlanta, and Birmingham. You are not a slave anymore. You don't have to live like this. Let me take you away from here.' I asked, 'Harvey, what would I do with my children?' He said, 'Take them. I will take care of them.' I said, 'But they are white children. What will people say? What will the laws do? What will people think? My children are as white as any children in this county.' He said, 'Millie, I love you. There has got to be a way.'

"Then, I discovered one morning that I was going to have a child by Harvey. I wondered what I was going to do. I was afraid to tell him. And I couldn't tell the colonel. So, Harvey had a birthday coming up. I wanted to fix him a birthday dinner.

"They had put some more room on my house. A room for the children, a room for me and the colonel, and a kitchen. Colonel George's wife had had an accident riding a horse. She fell off and broke her back. I had to take care of her and the little boy who had spells. I would cook and carry food to my children from the big house even though I did have a kitchen.

"I planned Harvey a birthday dinner. He never came until eleven or twelve o'clock at night. I told the colonel that I wasn't feeling very well that night, so I left early. I wanted to tidy up for Harvey. When the colonel came over that night, I told him I wasn't feeling well and I wanted to just lie down and get some rest. It seemed to bother him but he did leave.

"When he left I got my center table and put it in my bedroom. I decorated it and put all the food on the table, lit a candle, and about eleven o'clock I put the light out in the window. This was Harvey's signal to come on. He had a special way of knocking so that I would know who it was. He would always knock on my window—not on the door. I would go to the door and let him in. That night I had put on a beautiful kimono that ole man George's wife had once given me for Christmas. It had flowers on it and was beautiful. My hair was combed as you saw it when you got here tonight. I got some perfume that the colonel had given me and I put it on. Uncle Aaron's wife had put holes in my ears and I usually had straws in them. On this night I was wearing the earrings that Harvey had given me. I had everything set and I was going to tell him that I was going to have his baby. I then heard the knock on my window. I quickly lit the candle and almost ran to the door to meet the man I loved.

"I opened the door and he was clean. He had on starched and ironed pants; he had shaved; he had on a blue shirt, which was unbuttoned at the top and smelled like Saaman soap. I couldn't wait for him to take me in his arms. I said, 'surprise, surprise, happy birthday.' And he said, 'Honey, this is so sweet of you.'

"I had a present on the table wrapped for him. And I said we'll eat first and then you can open your present. I had no idea that colonel was watching my house that night. I think he had finally gotten suspicious of how I was acting. Just as we were about to sit down to eat, I heard the lock turning in the door. The colonel had a key to the house, and he opened the door and saw the whole picture. His face was as red as a tomato. He said, 'So this is what's going on. This is why you have been acting so funny. You got a nigger lover. But you won't have him for long.' He had a pistol in his hand. He said to Harvey, 'Get out of this house right now. By God I mean get out and get away from this farm tonight and I don't ever want to see you back here again.'

Colonel George stood there with that big six-shooter in his hand and with raging eyes said, "You are a damn Yankee, a hypocrite who thought you could fool us all, but didn't. If you want to ever see your buddies again, you get out of here, and get out right now.'

"'Yes, I joined the Union Army and risked my life to save people like Emily from southern slavery, and I am ready to risk my life again to save her from your so-called Master Georgeship,' Harvey replied.

"That remark seemed to make Colonel madder, and he said, 'Get out of here right now before I pull this trigger and blow you to hell—and you will take your dead hero John Brown's body.'

"Harvey retorted, 'It's too bad he didn't will you his soul.'

"Colonel George said, 'Listen, I've had enough, Jimbo. I'm

cocking this gun, and if you don't get out of here after I count to three, I'm going to pull the trigger—and I don't mean maybe.'

"When he cocked the gun, the silence in the room was so hard you couldn't cut it with a butcher's knife. The silence was broken only by the ticking of my little alarm clock on the table by my bed. It had both hands on twelve as if it was hiding its face from what was going on. It was then I cried out to Harvey, 'Please go, please. You can't do me or anybody else any good if you're dead. Give tomorrow a chance.'

"Colonel George said, 'I'm counting. ONE.' He paused a moment as Harvey just stood there. When he said 'TWO,' I started crying and shouting, 'Please, don't do this to me. I can't see you die.'

"Harvey turned then and walked slowly toward the door, never once giving us a backward glance, opening the door, walking out, and slamming it so hard I heard the key fall on the wood floor.

"Colonel George stood facing me. Even though my little coal oil lamp was burning, I could not see his face clearly, but I could tell by his voice that he was really mad. He had the gun in his hand, but suddenly I was not afraid of him. I guess I was too ... what is the word? Mr. Webb sometimes uses a word ... I think, *agonized*. Is that a good word, Professor Love?"

"Yes, ma'am," Professor Love answered. "I think it would be correct for expressing your feelings."

"The candle that lay on the floor was still lit and was burning a hole in my matted rug. Colonel George stepped up and stomped the fire out with his foot.

"He said to me, 'Did he tell you that he was a damn Yankee? I searched and found this out,' he said.

"I said, 'Why didn't you tell him?'

"He said, 'I wasn't afraid of telling him.'

"I said sarcastically, 'And maybe you should have told him that you stole my virginity. I was a virgin you know when your papa gave me to you.'

"He answered, 'If you want to know it, I was a virgin too or whatever a man is supposed to be who has never had sex with a woman.'

"I looked him straight in the eye and asked, 'Do you expect me to believe that?'

"He said, 'It's true, Millie, I swear, it's true.'

"And I replied, 'And maybe you should have told him that

31

you had the privilege of sleeping with two women—one a beloved red-headed wife and the other a concubine maid.'

"He said, 'You are angry and you know what we meant to each other before my wife ever came along.'

"I said, 'If you will please leave, I'll clean up and go to bed.'

"He replied, 'I'm sorry if you are mad with me, but I will put all of this broken glass and dishes in the trash and I will buy you a brand new tablecloth, dishes, and glasses to replace what I broke.'

"To this I replied, 'You don't have to George, after all it's yours in the first place. This is your house. You have a key to come and go as you please. You don't have to knock. My children belong to you, I belong to you, so I don't own anything—not even myself.'

"He laid his gun, which was still in his hand, down on the bed. He opened the door and picked up the key off the floor, which had fallen out when Harvey slammed it so hard. He laid the key on the bed and said, 'From now on I will knock when I come to your door because I am turning in the key. You will have a choice of letting me in or forbidding me.' He came over to where I was still standing and put his hand on my shoulder and I said, 'Please just leave me alone and go home.'

"He turned, picked up the tablecloth filled with the broken pieces by its four corners, opened the door, and said, 'Goodnight.'

"I locked the door and with my kimono with the satin collar still on, I laid down on the bed. After a while, I fell asleep.

"About two o'clock that night I was awakened by a familiar tap on my window. It could only be one person—the man I loved, Harvey. In the dark I pulled the curtain back and raised the window and he said, 'This is me.' I said, 'You shouldn't have come back. Your life is in danger. The colonel will shoot you.'

He replied, 'I have a gun, remember when they made one gun they made two. Come out here. I want to talk to you.'

"I quickly opened the door, picked up my key, and walked around on the dark side of the house where he was. He said, 'Lock your door and let's go down to Uncle Aaron's bunkhouse.' The bunkhouse was near the feedlot where he and Uncle Aaron rested during the day at dinnertime or when it was raining or cold.

"I locked the door and we hurriedly walked in the dark to the bunkhouse. Johnie's dog was walking right beside me. Nobody dared bother me unless he knew the person or he would tear them up. After entering the bunkhouse, Harvey closed the door and there in the darkness he said, 'Millie I came back after you. I want you to leave with me tonight.'

"But I protested, 'I can't leave my children. They are the only things that I have. I have no brothers, no sisters, my momma is dead, so I cannot dare to leave my children.'

"'Then take them with you,' he said.

"'Harvey, do you expect me to wake my children up at this time of night and leave? Where will you take them?' I asked.

"'We'll go up north,' he said. 'I did tell you, remember, I was from the north.'

"'Yes,' I said. 'And the colonel knows it too.'

"It was probably four o'clock in the morning when we parted. He walked me back to the house. The dog faithfully followed him. And he said, 'Millie, darling, are you sure you are not going to change your mind?'

"'Harvey,' I said, 'I love you but I love my children. And if I have to make a choice . . . Please try to understand. I'll have to make the children my choice.'

"For the last time, there in the dark, he took me in his arms and said, 'Goodbye Millie.' With tears in my eyes and in my throat and in my heart, I said, 'Goodbye, Harvey.' I never saw him again.

"The next day I walked around as if in a daze. George left me alone for the most part. He only said things to me when he had to. Three days later, I decided I could not live with this situation. I decided to kill myself. I took a handful of pills and almost died. Uncle Aaron found me lying on my bed. He heard me moaning and groaning. The children had gone riding their horses, and Uncle Aaron went quickly and got his wife. She was a midwife and that day my baby was aborted. I was sick for about a month. George took care of me. He hired one of the girls in the quarters to work in my place and still paid me my small salary. He bought medicine and anything that he thought I might want. After about a month I went back to work.

"I started going down to the quarters in my spare time taking the children with me because I wanted them to be with other colored children and know how they lived. I ran with the kids, I jumped rope, I played ball, and that's when they started calling me 'Aunt Millipus' because they said I was as sharp and swift as a cat.

"When Johnie was about sixteen years old, Colonel George

told me he wanted to talk to me. He told me to come upstairs to his office. His wife could no longer go upstairs because she was in a wheelchair.

"I went up the stairs to his office and he said to me, 'Millie, you are a good woman. A brave woman and I know that your life might have been different had I not interfered with it. I want in some small way to repay you for what you have meant in my life and for whatever I did that was unfair to you. A few weeks ago I went to East Texas and I bought 200 acres of land for you and our children. I want them to have a home of their own when I am gone. My wife and my son have this plantation of over 4,000 acres and all my livestock will go to them, but I want Johnie and Jeannie Mae and you to have a home of your own.'

"He pulled out some papers from a black bag and said, 'Here are the deeds to the land. It's in your name and the children's names too. You will be the guardian until these children are twenty-one years old. I went to the Cherokee County courthouse there and made arrangements for the taxes to be paid every year out of an account I opened up at a bank in Texas. In this bag there are some more things that I want you to have. I am going to put this bag up in the attic in the small trunk and lock it. I have two keys. I'm giving you one and I'll keep the other, but I don't want you to bother this stuff unless something happens to me.'

"I said, 'What's going to happen to you?' He replied, 'Well, I have sort of a bad heart.'

"He said, 'Just in case, I am going to ask you one request. If I die, don't leave my wife and son until they can make the adjustment. They would be completely lost without me and you. This may sound hard, but I am asking you this; it's all I'm asking you. Stay with them for at least six months.'

"I said, 'You love her don't you colonel?' He said, 'Just do this for me, and if I never say it again, thank you for what you have been in my life and forgive me if I have caused you hurt. But I cannot tell the truth if I deny loving you and these my children. Now leave me Millie, I just want to be alone.'

"As I came out of his room I got a glimpse of Aaron going down the stairs and I wondered if he heard the conversation because he was good at eavesdropping. As a matter of fact, he knew all the happenings in that house because he listened when he was serving parties or whenever there was company. He was a wise old man.

"About six months later Colonel George's wife heard a gunshot upstairs. Uncle Aaron and I also heard the shots and ran to see what was wrong. When we went upstairs we found the colonel lying on the bed. He had killed himself. It was a shock to all of us. My children took his death hard for he had bought them what they needed, sent them to school, even carried them to town with him and nobody bothered them because they were Colonel George's children. I remembered my promise but I didn't realize that this was to come so soon. True to my word I stayed on.

"Colonel George's wife had a brother, named Jeff Reynolds, who lived in Shreveport, and she sent for him to come and run the plantation. Now the colonel had what is known as a 'straw boss'—a white man who lived at the edge of the quarters. He didn't live in a cabin but in a nice white frame house. He was not the best man in Louisiana, and he tried to stick his nose in all the colored folks business and run back to tell Colonel George.

"So Jeff Reynolds came to run the plantation. I didn't like his attitude. He was bossy and wanted my children to work in the cane and cotton fields. I flat refused to obey his wishes because they never had done this in their lives. He sort of picked on Johnie, and one day I told him flatly, 'I don't have to stay here. I can go whenever I please. I am not a slave. I am a free woman.' He said, 'No, Millie, I don't want you to go. You have been too much of a help with my sister.'

"Later on Mrs. Jackson seemed to have gotten worse. They heard of a doctor in Atlanta who they believed could help her. So Mrs. Jackson and her son caught the train and went to Atlanta to stay with their distant cousins and take treatments from this doctor.

"One evening, about three weeks after they had gone, I was out in the kitchen garden when I heard noises. When I looked up, Jeannie Mae came running to me crying with her clothes half torn off. I hurriedly went to her and asked what was the trouble. What she said shocked me. Jeff Reynolds had sexually attacked her. Uncle Aaron was out back and both of us started running toward the big house. Jeannie Mae said that Johnie and Jeff Reynolds were upstairs fighting. Uncle Aaron and I ran in the house and up the stairs. Johnie and Jeff Reynolds were down on the floor. Johnie's hand was bleeding and Jeff Reynolds was bleeding behind his ear. A butcher knife lay about two feet from them, and Johnie was pounding Jeff Reynolds face with his fist. The smell of whiskey was strong in the room, and I knew that Jeff had been back to his old habits of drinking. Uncle Aaron and I pulled them apart.

"Uncle Aaron said, 'Millie, take that boy downstairs and wash that blood off of his hand. I'll take care of Cap'n Reynolds. He'll be all right.'

"I took Johnie downstairs and washed the cut on his hand and bandaged it up. Meanwhile Uncle Aaron took care of Cap'n. He was cussing and using all kinds of bad words. He called Johnie a damn half-breed. Uncle Aaron poured some whiskey in the glass and made Cap'n Reynolds drink it.

"He said to me, 'He'll be drunk now for a few hours, but when he becomes sober he'll want to kill that boy. Whatever he tells the law they are going to believe it 'cause the law is going to believe a white man. So Millie you need to get that boy out of here tonight. If Cap'n Reynolds can't do it by himself, he might get him a mob crowd and kill that boy. I ain't going to tell you nothing wrong. We need to get Johnie off of this place tonight.' Johnie didn't want to go. He said, 'I ain't scared of him. I ain't scared of Jeff Reynolds. He raped my sister, and I'll kill him.'

"Uncle Aaron said, 'Son, you can't fight white folks. I'm telling you for good. You get off this plantation tonight. I got a boy down in the quarters that will help you get away. He knows this delta like a book. He knows people in other quarters. He knows our sign we give each other for help and he'll get you out of here. When this all blows over, maybe you can come back and get your momma and sister. But son, hear me. Millie, tell him. You get off this plantation tonight.'

"Uncle Aaron had his way. He saddled the horse while I went to the house and got Johnie a few clothes and put them in a flour sack. I went and ripped my bed mattress apart and got money that I had hid in that mattress. I gave some of it to Johnie. I said goodbye to my son. Then I decided I wasn't going to stay on the plantation another night. I told Jeannie Mae to put on some more clothes, and we got our clothes and put them in a bag. We wrapped the bag with cords, saddled the horse in the dark, and got the rest of my money out of the mattress.

"Then I thought about the black bag that Colonel Williams told me to get if I left the plantation. I went into the house and walking quietly up the stairs I peeped in the room where Jeff Reynolds was. He was still drunk and was snoring. I tiptoed up to the attic, took the key, and opened the door. There in the dark I took the key from around my neck to the trunk.

"I opened the trunk and there was the bag. I made sure I had lit a candle. I took the bag and closed the trunk back. I didn't take time to lock it nor to lock the attic door. I almost ran down the stairs with that bag in my hands. My daughter and I left, and I told her we were going to New Orleans. I didn't know how far it was. I had never been there, but I prayed the Lord would help me to get there.

"We rode all night. Early the next morning we came to another plantation. We went to the colored quarters and I used words and gave the sign that Uncle Aaron told my boy to use when you come to colored people. They accepted me. They took my horse and hid it. They fed us and put us to sleep. They fed the horse and gave us a room. It was a nice family of colored people. We had our clothes in our room and we had that black bag. I told the old man that I was trying to go to New Orleans, and he got another man to get his horse and go with us all the way to New Orleans.

"I had never seen a big town before in my life. It was a big city. The man helped me find the colored part of town. He also helped me find a lady who had a rooming house and two or three little rent houses. She ran a joint where people drank beer and ate barbecue and the like. She let us have a room that night. I told her I was looking for a place to stay, and she rented us a small house.

"The people seemed to have a problem with Jeannie Mae because she looked white. I had to assure them over and over that she was my daughter. The landlady asked me if I wanted to work. When I told her I had cooked all my life, she offered me a job working in what she called a 'cafe.'

"The house she rented to us had furniture, and after we sold the horse and got settled we opened the black bag for the first time. Sure enough in that bag were those deeds to that property in Texas with our names on it and $500 dollars cash money. I could hardly believe it. Colonel had left us that much money. I never had that much money in my life. We put the money back in the bag and hid it between mattresses.

"My landlady got my daughter a job washing and ironing for some white people. They would bring their clothes in a wicker basket, and Jeannie Mae would wash in a washtub and iron those clothes with a smoothing iron. The white folks had two boys, and her husband brought the clothes every Monday and came and picked them up on a Thursday. So we were both working.

"About six weeks later I discovered that Jeannie was going to have a baby. Jeff Reynolds had gotten her pregnant that evening when he raped her. My fifteen-year-old baby was going to have a baby. I was very upset. I thought about asking my landlady, who was a midwife, if could she throw the baby away, but then I said no. Suppose my child died. I would have nobody.

"So about eight months later Jeannie Mae had her baby. I can't explain it. The moment I saw the baby I loved it. It was a little girl. I loved her. Even though she was as white as any white person, I knew she was still my grandchild. I was really proud of her. But I didn't show my affection too much around Jeannie Mae. Oh, I would feed her. Jeannie Mae nursed her on her breast. I gave her a sugar tit. I would bathe her and when Jeannie wasn't around I would kiss her, even on her bottom. I would rub her down. I bought baby powders, cuddled her in my arms, and called her sweet names. But when her mother was around, I did not display this type of attitude, and Jeannie Mae thought I didn't like her baby. But I loved her. So one day I took the baby to a man that put tattoos on people's bodies because I wanted her marked in a way that if anybody took her I would know her by that tattoo on her thigh. I had them put an 'X' on her left thigh and then I had him put one on my left thigh in the same place. So if anything ever happened to my grandbaby this 'X' would be how I would identify her.

"Jeannie named the baby Queen Victoria because she said she was a little queen. We called her 'Queenie.' When little Queenie was about a year and a half old, I went home one evening from work and found a note on my bed saying 'Momma, Queenie and I are gone. Thank you for all you have done for us, but I know you didn't care for my baby and I thought it best that we would leave and start a life of our own. I love you. Jeannie Mae.'

"I didn't know what to do. I was shocked. The only two people I had were now gone. I wondered if she went to the white folks because they were white. Or did she go to the black folks. I went back down to my landlady's house because she knew a lot of people in New Orleans. As a matter of fact she was supposedly a fortuneteller. I offered to pay her if she could find my child and her baby. She had connections and she got right on

38

the case. But they didn't know where to look. She could not look in her crystal ball and tell me where my child and grandchild were. I think I almost lost my mind. No matter where I looked I found no trace of her. So I went on living by myself, praying every night, 'Lord, please take care of my child.' I spent a lot of time with my landlady because I hated to go to that house by myself. I went with her when she delivered babies. I learned how to be a midwife. She tried to teach me voodoo, and I listened and almost halfway believed in it.

"And then about a year and a half later one night I was in my bed and heard a knock on my door.

"I said, 'Who is that?' The voice said, 'It's me, Momma, Jeannie Mae.' I sprang out of bed and unlocked the door. I opened the door and there stood my child. I was crying. We were both crying. We were in each other's arms. I said, 'Jeannie Mae, you feel hot, what's the matter?'

"She said, 'Momma I'm sick.' I said, 'Come on, come on. Lie down. Here, give me your bag.' I took her suitcase, sat it down against the wall, laid her down, and pulled off her clothes.

"She said, 'Give me some water.' I gave her some water. I rubbed her and then I couldn't wait to ask her, 'Where is Queenie?' She said, 'Momma, can we talk about that tomorrow. I'm sick and I don't feel like talking about that now. Just let me rest. I'm tired.'

"The next day I got my landlady to get a doctor to come to the house to see Jeannie Mae. He told me that she had tuberculosis and there was nothing he could do for her. About two days later I had to know. 'Jeannie Mae,' I said, 'where is Queenie? Tell me what happened to little Queenie?' She said, 'Momma, I guess I gave her away.'

"What do you mean, I guess? You guess you gave her away? Who did you give her too? This is the story she told me.

'Momma, I always felt that you didn't like my baby Victoria. Even though the way it happened, I wished it could have happened differently. But still I loved my baby. So I decided that I would just go away somewhere and start my life in another place. Thanks to you I saved my money. So while you were gone I packed my clothes, caught the train, and went to a place called Lake Charles, Louisiana, which is the parish seat of Calcasieu Parish. I got off the Southern Pacific train, which goes from New Orleans to Lake Charles to Houston. I had a hackney driver take me to the colored part of town. He looked at me and hesitated because he thought I was a white woman. I had to reassure him again and again that I was a colored woman before he would take me to a rooming house, which an elderly black woman ran. I again had a problem convincing her that my baby and I were colored. After she was convinced, she gave me a room upstairs and let me use her kitchen. She was a nice old lady and she helped me find a job doing housework for a wealthy white family. The family lived about a mile and a half from the rooming house. She kept my baby for me, and I cooked and cleaned house five days a week and walked the distance there and back each day.

"One day I was walking home from work and there came a driving rain. It rains a lot in Lake Charles. But on this day I got almost soaking wet about halfway home. It was raining so hard I stopped at a fish market that a black man owned. I asked him if I could stay until the rain slowed up. He was very nice to me. He said he had seen me often pass this place. He ran a domino shack in the back and offered to take me home in his cart. I thanked him but refused. He gave me an umbrella, and I went on home. After that we always spoke whenever I passed his place and finally we started a friendship. He later asked me if he could come to the rooming house to visit me. I was hesitant and asked him if he had a wife. He said no. He was unmarried. He was about thirty-two years old. I told him I would have to ask my landlady if it was all right. Then I would let him know. She said it was perfectly all right. We would sit on her front porch and just talk. He would bring my baby candy and toys. Finally, we took walks up and down the streets, and he was very nice. After a while he asked me to marry him. I told him I had to think about this. He told me that he would be able to take care of the baby and me, and that if I became his wife I would not have to work anymore unless I wanted to help him in the meat market. Later I found out that he killed a calf every Friday, cut it up, and sold briskets, steaks, and other parts of the cow. Anyway, I finally consented to marry him.

"'He rented a two-bedroom house, took me to a furniture store, and helped me select new furniture. This is something I had never done in my whole life. He was very kind and made me comfortable. He and Victoria loved each other. I helped him in the evening during busy hours and sometimes on Fridays. We would be at the market until eleven o'clock. The domino shack was closed about 9 o'clock at night. My husband had cat-

40

tle on a little farm outside of town and that's where he killed his calf. He kept money and bought me nice things—wedding ring, necklace, bracelets, and most any little thing I wanted. He was a good person to me. However, I was always a little afraid about him having so much money in his pocket and being at the shop late at night. I feared somebody might rob him.

"'My fears became a reality one night. While we were closing up and counting the money some men came into the shop to rob him. He fought them and tried to get to his gun, which was under the counter. Unfortunately, they beat him to it. I picked up a butcher knife and tried to help him. One of them threw me down, took the butcher knife, and hit me several times. He then took the gun and killed my husband. At this time I was about four months pregnant with his child and the experience did me so bad I lost the child. I buried him and wondered what I must do next. I stayed on for a few days in the house, but I was afraid. I closed the market, but I was never really well again after that. My health seemed to get worse, and I finally went to a doctor. He told me that I was in the first stage of tuberculosis, which they called 'TB.' He also told me that there was a city in Texas called San Antonio, which had a hospital where I might get some help. I sold my furniture and everything else that I could. I drew out the money we had left in the bank after funeral expenses.

"'I took my baby, bought a ticket, and caught the train for San Antonio. This time I rode in the white coach. I was so sick I did not argue with the porter or conductor that I was black. I just wanted to get on that train and go to San Antonio where I hoped to get some help. Everybody in the coach thought me and little Victoria were white. I was not trying to be white. I really just wanted to be left alone. But it seems I got worse on the train.

"'There was a young white couple sitting right across the aisle from me, and they discovered that I was sick. So they were very nice to me. They had food and gave some to Victoria. They helped me so much with Victoria. They even had aspirin that they gave me because I had fever. When I went to sleep they took Victoria. She took to them, too. But my situation seemed to get worse. Finally, they told me that they were on their way to San Antonio and suggested that I let them keep Victoria until I found me a place to stay and see a doctor. They gave me an address where they would be and assured me that they would take care of the baby. Whenever I wanted her I could come and get her.

"Jeannie Mae said, 'Momma, you have to understand that I was a real sick person and I was in no shape to take care of the baby. So I agreed to let them keep the baby.'

"Jeannie Mae continued the story. 'I took their address and their name. I guess I was a little afraid that they might not be telling the truth. So when we got to San Antonio, I paid the porter $2 to find out if that was their name and if that was where they were going. He told me that their real names were Walter and Marie Webb. That was the name that they had given me. I kept the address and the name, but the porter also told me that that was not their final destination. They were really on their way to a place called Koohne Town. The doctors thought I was a white woman, and they found me a place to stay.

"'After two days, I had a driver take me to this house where the Webbs were staying. When I arrived no one was there. When I asked the people next door about some visitors to that place, they told me that the owners were at work and they had company, but the company had left the day before. They didn't know where they had gone.

"'It seemed that I got sicker after that. I don't know if it was because I had lost Victoria or if it was my health. I caught the train and came back to New Orleans where you were. The doctor told me that I could not live, but I hope that one day, if I die, maybe you might find little Victoria. The name of this couple and the name of the town is all in my pocketbook. That's all I know.' This was the end of Jeannie Mae's story.

"Two days later Jeannie died. I couldn't bring myself to tell even the old lady I worked for the story about the baby and what Jeannie had been through. I just didn't want to talk about it. I buried her in the community cemetery there in New Orleans.

"Now I had no known relatives except a little two and a half or three-year-old grandbaby somewhere in Texas. I hated to go home that night from work. So I stayed on the job and helped Momma Jane who was supposed to have been a fortuneteller and a midwife. I helped her deliver babies. She even taught me things she called magic. She taught me how to take roots and make medicine and read palms. She even gave me a crystal ball, but she said you had to have a gift to do this. Anyway, it was something to keep my mind from thinking about my little granddaughter. When I went home at night I was so tired I just went to bed. But I could not get little Queen Victoria out of my mind. Finally, I decided I was going to try to find her. It was then that I told Momma Jane the rest of the story. That is, I told her that Jeannie had given the baby away. I did not tell her where or about Texas. I just told her that she had given the baby away while she was gone. Then I asked if she could look into her crystal ball and tell me where the baby was. I was desperate. She said, 'Millie, this may be hard, but I'll see what I can do.'

Momma Jane sort of went off into a trance. She turned the lights down real low in the room, put on some kind of kimono, and tied a scarf around her head. She completely ignored me and began to look into the crystal ball. I watched with curiosity and a little fear because she seemed to have transformed herself into some kind of wizard. Finally, she said, 'Millie, I see that your grandbaby has gone toward the setting sun. You will go far in that direction. I see you at a place and I see a black man coming toward you. He has a pack on his back. I cannot see his name. I just see an 'L', that's all. You will follow that man and you will find your grandchild.'

"I went to the store and bought a big suitcase. I packed my clothes and got the black bag that had the money in it and the deeds. I put my daughter's jewelry, her beautiful necklace and rings, and her marriage license in the trunk. I also put my best clothes in there. The rest I gave to Momma Jane.

"I went to the train station and bought a ticket for Lake Charles. I got off the train and had a hackney driver take me to this rooming house that I had from where my daughter first lived. I told the woman who I was and about my child and my grandchild, and she accepted that I was telling the truth. She said my daughter sold the furniture in the house, and she kept part of the money for when Jeannie would come back. I showed her the death certificate, and she gave me Jeannie's half of the money. The next day I caught the train for San Antonio, Texas. When I got off the train with my big suitcase and a handbag, I didn't know what to do next. I had the address of this place in San Antonio where these people had spent a couple of days and I had the names of Walter and Marie Webb and the place called Koohne Town. That's all I had. I had traveled west toward the setting sunset just like Momma Jane said.

"As other people met friends and loved ones, I stood there alone beside the train, wondering what to do next."

Lazarus

"I was about to sit down on my suitcase when I looked about 100 yards and I saw a black man walking in my direction. When he turned to look back from where he was coming, I discovered that he had a pack on his back and then it came to me what Momma Jane had said. He was a black man and he came walking slowly toward me. When he got there, he asked me if someone was supposed to meet me and didn't show up. I told him no. I was looking for some folks that didn't live here. He asked me where these people lived.

"'Do they live in Texas?' he asked.

"I said, 'Yes they do as far as I know.' I discovered that he was a tramp and I was a little suspicious of him.

He asked me, 'What's the name of the town that you are looking for?'"

"I said, 'Koohne Town.'

"He looked funny at me. He asked, 'Is that where you want to go? Lady, I know exactly where that is. That's in East Texas. You are a long way from Koohne Town. That's my center home.

'Look,' he said, 'I'm a tramp, a hobo. I ride the freight train all the way from California and back. But I'm on my way to Koohne Town. That's my second home when I ain't riding the train. And if you want to go, and you ain't 'fraid to ride a freight train, we can get in boxcars, and I'll take you to Koohne Town. Who in Koohne Town are you looking for?'

"I asked, 'Do you know anybody in Koohne Town named Webb?'"

"'Sure,' he said, 'Well I know Webb. He don't live in town but he lives outside of town. Old man Walter Webb. But he died. A year or two ago his son came and took over his farm after his father died. Now, he's white folks. Are these white or black folks you are looking for?'

"I said, 'All I know is that it's some Webbs in Koohne Town that I am looking for. That's all I can tell you.'

"He said, 'If you are not afraid to ride on a freight train, I'll take your suitcase and put it on an empty boxcar and I'll show you. We'll go together. I'm on my way.'

"I said to him, 'Look if you will help me find Koohne Town, I'll buy you a ticket. I've never rode a freight train. I'll buy you a ticket.'

"He said, 'Lady, I don't have no money to ride a passenger train.'

"I said, 'I'm going to buy you a ticket to ride.'

"He said, 'All right. It's a deal.'

"He took my suitcase and I took the handbag and we went into the train station to the colored section. I went to the ticket window and told the agent I wanted two one-way tickets to Koohne Town, Texas. He looked at some papers of a map and told me how much they would be. I gave him the money, went back, and gave the man one of the tickets. Then I asked him, 'And what is your name?'

"He said, 'Lazarus.'

"'Lazarus what?' I asked.

"'Just Lazarus,' he answered.

"And then I remembered what Momma Jane said, 'All I can see is an 'L.'

"So maybe even if I didn't have a lot of faith in this kind of voodoo reading, maybe it's something to this. I'm going to follow this man.

"And then he asked me, 'What's your name?'

"I said, 'Millie.'

"He said, 'Millie what?'

"I replied, 'Millipus, Aunt Millipus.'

"'And that's all of your name,' he asked.

"I said, 'Just call me Aunt Millipus.'

Millipus got up out of her rocking chair and got her a drink of water. She looked at Professor Love and Jay and asked, "Are you all tired of listening to this? Have you heard enough?"

Professor Love said, "No, Aunt Millie. It's very interesting. I want to hear the rest of it."

She asked, "What about you Jay?"

Jay replied, "I'm all ears Aunt Millipus. Go ahead with your story."

She sat back down in her chair, folded her arms across her chest, leaned back, closed her eyes, and continued on again.

"We came to Koohne Town about four o'clock in the evening. We got off the train and Lazarus said, 'This is it. This is Koohne Town. See that sign up there saying Koohne Town?'

"I said, 'That's a funny name.'

"'Well,' he said, 'it was an old settler years ago that came in here and staked off thousands of acres of land and his name was Koohne. And he built up most of the town. There was a lot of coons in this area, and I don't know whether that was his name but it was spelled differently. It was spelled K-O-O-H-N-E. He built a trading store here, sold groceries, bought animal hides and sold them, and started this town. When he died he had one son named Richard. Richard Koohne had a saloon, lumberyard, started a post office, and got the school going. They named the town Koohne Town.'

"The main street divided the town. On the other side of the street was the county seat. It was all the same town but divided by the highway.

"He said, 'Old man Richard Koohne is one of the richest men in East Texas. He is known all the way from Austin. The governor knows him. In fact, they know Richard Koohne in Washington, D.C. He is a powerful man in this area. He always has his way. One time they would not let him have his way. This was when the school organized a ball team. They did not want to be called coons. That's what they used to call us. They didn't want to be called the Koohne Town Coons. This is what they did. Old man Koohne had married a lady from the East. I think she was from Philadelphia and her first name was Angela. So they discussed it and decided to name the ball team the Koohne Town Angels after old man Koohne's wife. Old man Koohne went for that and said, 'What difference will it make a hundred years from now?' But come on let's come on to the store. I have a few nickels and I can buy us something to eat.'

"We walked up the railroad track and across the street to a store called Koohne Mercantile. We walked in the store and the storekeeper said, 'Well, I be damned, here's Lazarus. Where in hell did you come from?' he asked.

"'Well, like I always said, I don't let no grass grow under my feet. I move around,' Lazarus replied.

"The storekeeper said, 'It's been a year or more since I last saw you. Is this your wife?'

"Lazarus said, 'No I ain't got no wife.'

"'Who is she Lazarus, what's her name?' the storekeeper asked.

"Lazarus replied, 'Her name is Aunt Millipus.'

"The storekeeper said, 'That's a strange name.'

"Lazarus said, 'Well, that's her name. Now give me some sausage, crackers, and cheese.'

"He cut us up some sausage and gave us cheese and crackers in a paper sack. I paid for it. We went out and sat on a bench on the front porch and ate. A black man came to town in a wagon and Lazarus said, 'Now that wagon is from the area where the colored folks live. The crossroads is about five miles from here, and I'm going to get him to let us ride.'

"We stood up and I said to him, 'Lazarus, I want you to do me a favor. Would you?'

"'Yes,' he said, 'if I can. You bought me a ticket here. I never rode on a passenger train in my life. What do you want me to do?'

"I said, 'I want you to promise me that you will never tell anybody that I mentioned the Webbs to you.' He looked at me strangely.

"He said, 'Millipus, I think you know something. But I won't ask you any more questions. I promise, cross my heart (as he made a cross with his right hand over his heart). I raise my hand to God and swear I won't tell it unless you ask me.'

"After he swore that he would never tell anybody, the church bell immediately began to chime and Lazarus said, 'It's five o'clock. Ole man Richard Webb gave those chimes to the church when they built it and everyday at five o'clock that song you hear is played. Do you know what it is?' He answered his own question by saying, "'That's *My Country 'Tis of Thee.*'

"We rode back to the crossroads in the wagon, and when we got there Lazarus took my suitcase in one hand and his pack on his back as we both went to Deacon Moses Randolph's store that was at the corner of Crossroads and Sandy Lane.

"Since it was in the summertime, the days were long. Deacon Randolph's store was still open. With it being Saturday, he always stayed open later. When we walked into the store, Deacon Randolph said, 'Well, look who's here, Lazarus. Where in the world did you come from?'

"He said, 'Dek, look like that's what everybody wants to know. You know, I hear old Reverend Prince say one time right cross there at that church, he said, the Lord asked the devil where was he was going and the devil said I'm going up and down the earth seeing who I can destroy. You remember that? Now I ain't the devil and I ain't trying to destroy anybody, but I've been going up and down the earth. I hope that answered your question.'

"'All right, Lazarus, Deacon Randolph said, 'and who is this woman you got with you? Is this your sweetheart or something?'

"'Dek, this woman is from New Orleans and she's coming here looking for a place to live and work. Her name is Millipus, and she ain't my sweetheart. And I hope that answered that question.'

"'All right, Lazarus,' he said. 'Man, when God made you he didn't make another. He broke the mold.'

"'Now Dek,' Lazarus said, 'right over there at that church I hear Reverend Prince in that pulpit said that there was a beggar in the Bible and he was full of sores and went to the rich man's house and dogs licked his sores. So he had to make two Lazarus' at least. Do you remember that?'

"'O.K. Lazarus, I remember. Now, what do you want to do with this lady?'

"'Can you give her a place to stay for a while?' Lazarus asked. He added, 'She can cook, wash and iron, clean house, and do most anything.'

Deacon Randolph turned to me and said, 'Can you chop cotton?' I told him that I had never chopped in a cotton field but I chopped my garden and flowerbeds. So he said, 'Well, you can get a job around here chopping cotton.'

"Deacon Randolph told Lazarus to take me over to his house, right next door, and his wife Elizabeth would find me a place to sleep. Deacon Randolph walked out of the store ahead of us and called his wife and said, 'Lazarus is bringing a lady from Louisiana to stay. Try to fix up something for her.'

"Then he said, 'Lazarus, where you gonna stay?'

"Lazarus, turned and looked at him. 'Dek, right over there at the church house.'

"Deacon Randolph said, 'Not again, please.'

"'I'm just going to tell you what Reverend Prince said. He said that Jesus said the birds have nests, and the foxes have holes to stay in, and that Jesus said he didn't have nowhere to lay his head. Ain't we supposed to be like Jesus? So don't worry about me. Just take care of the lady.'

"Deacon Randolph shook his head and went back into the store. The Randolph's were nice to me. They helped me find work in the fields. I stayed with them for the rest of the summer.

"I joined the church and then one day, on the first of August when I went home from work, Miss Lizzie, who did not work in the fields, told me a lady came by the store trying to find somebody to work for her because she was going to start teaching school in Koohne Town. She said she had a little daughter who was about three years old, and this lady wanted to know if we knew anybody who would want to cook, wash and iron, clean house, and take care of her three-year old child. Miss Lizzie told her that she did know a lady that might be interested. The lady told Miss Lizzie that she wanted to talk to me. Ms. Lizzie said to me, 'You probably never heard tell of this woman before. But her name is Marie Webb. She has plenty of money. I don't know why she wants to teach school. I know money ain't the reason.'

"The next day Ms. Marie Webb came to see me. I had to hide my excitement because perhaps this was the child I was looking for. She carried me to the house. It was a big house. It was a two-story white house and was sitting on a hill. It had a large windmill in the yard. She questioned me, and I told her that I had cooked and cleaned house all my life. I had also worked with children before. She hired me and told me I would be staying in the back yard in the servant's house. She said I could eat out of her kitchen and she would pay me $2.50 a week. Unfortunately, I didn't see the baby that day. She said she was upstairs sleep. But I could not wait to see her.

"When I moved in, the little girl came out in the yard where I was. She looked like Jeannie Mae and she also had the forehead just like Jeff Reynolds. She was the split image of him from her nose up. I could hardly wait to raise her and dress her to see if there was a tattoo on her left thigh. When I did undress her, there it was. My granddaughter, little Victoria. I could tell nobody because she was a white girl.

"I worked for the Webbs for over fifteen years. When I started having rheumatism, Victoria was grown. They bought me an acre and a half of land right across from the church. They gave me a mule and had a house moved onto the property. They deeded it to me because I was having rheumatism, and they gave me furniture and everything. They dug me a well and here I am right now.

"I rented a post office box and paid my taxes by mail on that place down in East Texas. I still had the deeds and I had the deed to the property that Walter and Marie Webb gave me and now I'm getting old and sick and Victoria is in college. She is going with one of the richest East Texas man's grandsons— Richard Koohne III. But she's my granddaughter. Now she's the only kinfolk I have in the world, and I want her to have what her grandfather, George Jackson, gave to her mother, her uncle, and me. I know she don't need the property, but it's family. She's all I have and I want her to have it. So 'Fessor Love, I want you to help me make out my will and give it—everything I have —to Victoria Webb. That's my story. Now again, I want you and Jay to promise me that you won't tell anybody what I've told you'll tonight."

'Fessor Love said, "Aunt Millipus, that is one of the most interesting stories I ever heard in my life. It sounds like something out of a storybook. But you can have my word I will not tell anyone. Not even my wife Geraldine unless you tell me sometime later to make it known."

Jason said, "Aunt Millipus, you have my word. I promise."

"Well," Professor Love said, "if that's all, we are going to go and let you go to bed. It's getting late."

"Thank you all for coming," said Aunt Millipus. "I do hope that my granddaughter will accept my will, but I wouldn't want her to be in a position for people to know that she was my granddaughter. I need to do this before I die."

As they were about to leave, she said, "Tell me something. What is Lazarus' last name? He was kind enough to bring me here. Is it just Lazarus?"

Jason and Professor Love looked at each other and Professor Love replied, "Uncle Frank Thomas told me that Lazarus and his grandpa were brought to Texas as slaves, and that when Lazarus was about fourteen years old he ran away and stayed until slavery was over. He came back to see his grandpa who went in the name of his former slave owner. Lazarus had changed his name but his name is really the name of the family slave owner. That owner, who is now dead, was Old man Jim Walter Webb. Lazarus' name is Lazarus Webb.

"Aw," she said, "now I see. Good night Professor and Jason."

Chapter 5

The Rebound

Jason gave serious thought to Aunt Millie's story, but he had problems of his own. He had to take over the family. He had to put schooling behind him. He went to work by plowing, chopping, grubbing stumps, and parttime working for Mrs. Winfield. He picked and sold berries, fished, sold fish, caught animals and sold hides. He was determined to keep his promise to his papa.

Then one day, when he was down in the pasture across from the road from him where he was hunting, he heard somebody screaming. He went to investigate what was wrong. He discovered that it was Violet. A white man named Claude was attacking her and trying to wrestle her to the ground. She was screaming and trying to fight him. Jason rushed to where they were and pulled them apart. He hit Claude with his fist and knocked him down. Claude sprang up, and a duel between them began.

As they were fighting, Uncle Sam Moore suddenly came up and shouted, "What are y'all doing? Cut it out, right now I said. Cut it out." They separated. Each was puffing and blowing. Uncle Sam said, "What's going on? What's this all about?"

Violet replied, "I was down here picking berries Papa, and this white man grabbed me and tried to throw me down."

Claude replied, "No, Uncle Sam, she ain't telling you the truth. I walked up on her and Jason all hugged up, and he was kissing her. And I told him I was going to tell you. And then he jumped on me."

Jason said, "That's not true. You know you were attacking Violet. She's telling the truth, Uncle Sam."

Claude said, "You see his gun over there don't you? He jumped on me 'cause I said I was going to tell on you."

Uncle Sam said to Jason, "You lowdown, dirty black coon. You're lying, I told you to stay away from my daughter. I know this white man ain't lying. White folks don't have to lie. I told you to let my daughter alone."

He picked up the gun and said, "I got a good mind to shoot you right now."

Violet was crying. She said, "Papa, Claude's not telling you the truth."

Papa said, "Shut up, girl. You just wait till I get you home."

He turned and said to Jason, "I ain't going to shoot you. But you will never forget this day." He took Jason's gun. He took the load out of it, hit it on a stump, and broke the handle off of the barrel. He threw it to Jason and said, "Now git off from here and never let me catch you with my daughter again."

Jason picked up the two pieces of his gun and started back home. As he walked, he wondered . . . What else could happen to him? Who could he talk to? Not his momma. She was expecting the baby any day now. He thought about Aunt Millipus. But she had her own problems. He thought about talking to Uncle Frank Cotton. But he knew just about what he would say because Uncle Frank Cotton was afraid of white folks. And then there was his friend Mose. What would Mose say? He would probably say, "Go get your daddy's gun and blow Claude's brains out." So Jason decided to just keep it to himself.

It was about a week later when late one evening Mose came to see him. He said, "Come out here. I need to talk to you." They went out to the barn and Mose said, "I have a letter here from Violet. She told me to give it to you."

He took the letter with trembling hands. He unfolded it and began to read. In it she said how sorry she was for what had happened in the pasture and thanked him from the bottom of her heart for rescuing her when otherwise she would had been raped by a white man. "It just made me love you more," she wrote. "I have to stop now," she wrote. "Papa is coming and he's got some plans for me." She signed it "YKW," which meant, "you-know-who."

Jason looked at Mose and said, "She says Uncle Sam has some plans for her. Do you know what they are?"

"Yes, I do," Mose replied. "You know that Violet's momma is my nanny. That's my momma's sister—Nanny Clara. And they got a sister named Dora that lives in Chicago. Uncle Sam had them to write my auntie in Chicago and to ask if Violet could come up there to live and go to school. My auntie wrote right back and told her yes and sent her a ticket for Violet to come to Chicago to live with her and her husband. That's the plan. They are getting ready right now to put her on the train. It ain't Nanny Clara's idea; it's Uncle Sam's. Nanny Clara don't want her to go. But she's going to do whatever Uncle Sam says."

"Well," sighed Jason, "If that's the way it is, it's nothing I can do."

Mose replied, "There is something that you can do."

"What?" Jason asked.

Mose said, "Marry her. You two can run off. You love her, and she loves you. You are nineteen and she is seventeen. Marry her."

Jason thought about it and said, "But Mose, I have my mother to take care of. My brothers and sisters. The farm. I couldn't ask her to come and live with me."

"Look," Mose replied, "if you really want the girl, you will find the way. Once you marry her, she's your wife. Ain't nothing Uncle Sam can do."

"Mose, it just can't be done that way. There must be another way," Jason replied.

"There is another way, Jason. Let her go. They can put her on the train, but she can get off at the next station if she wants to. I will tell you this. God knows I love Nanny Clara, but I wouldn't give a quarter for Uncle Sam. And Violet is my first cousin. But if they are going to go along with Uncle Sam, let them go. I wouldn't want to be in a family where they wouldn't want me. Man, there are plenty of pretty looking girls from here to all the way to Red Bluff. Girls would be glad to have a guy like you. Man, I wouldn't let them run me crazy. Go and find you somebody else. I'm talking about my cousin."

Jason went to the train station that day when Violet caught the train. He stood afar off and waved bood-by to her from a distance.

His mother's baby came about a week later. He went and got Aunt Millipus to deliver the child. They called him little Wade.

About the middle of May the community, as always, started making plans for the nineteenth of June celebration. It was a very patriotic and enthusiastic occasion. However, Jason had to think about the funeral of his father, which was to be held on the second Sunday in July. People came from near and far to the forestated funeral.

It was in August that Uncle Frank Cotton's niece came to the Crossroad community. She was a very good-looking young woman. She was about twenty-three years old. She was graceful and well dressed. She had lost her husband and came to stay with Uncle Frank and his family for awhile. She had been living in Memphis.

One night the week before she came, the Baptist church burned to the ground. Without a doubt, in one person's mind, the Klan was responsible. The people in the community felt that the church was burned because it was a combination of the enthusiastic celebration on the nineteenth of June and the colored people getting ready to stand up for their rights. What made it more real to them was that the community had just had another meeting in the Baptist church about them sticking together and about getting the school trustees to build another room on the school and hire a third teacher. The school board said that it didn't have any money to build another room. So all the big Crossroad colored people all the way down in the bottom had a meeting to raise money and have a room built themselves. Then the church burned.

Even the white people all the way up to Koohne Town were disturbed about this. Old man Koohne came down and had a meeting with the colored people and told them that he would get to the bottom of this incident even if he had to go to Austin or to Washington, D.C.

Mr. Koohne said, "We're not going to have no Klan coming into our community bothering us. You people work for us. I loan y'all money, and you buy stuff from me to help me make a living. You got your church and school and we got our church and our school; you go to yours and we go to ours. You celebrate your nineteenth of June and we celebrate our 4th of July. Ain't nobody going to come in here and tear up our community. I'm giving warning. I'm going to help y'all build your church back.

I'm a deacon at my church and I'll see to you getting some money. I know those folks can get you some money. You'll have church in the schoolhouse. If y'all want to make a note, some of you got a farm and some livestock, so come up to my bank and I'll let y'all have some money. Keep doing what you are doing because what difference will it make a hundred years from now?"

It would seem ironic that Uncle Frank's niece would come in at this time. Since school didn't start until October, they had raised enough money to build a room on the school and the school board agreed to hire Leola as a primary teacher.

The Methodist church, which held church services only two Sundays in the month, offered the Baptist church their facilities for the other two Sundays for their services. The churches had a good relationship.

It was late one August evening that Mose went to Jason's house. Jason could tell that Mose had excitement in his eyes.

Mose said, "Man I've got some news for you."

"And what is it?" Jason asked.

He said, "Come on, let's go out to the barn and talk. I don't want nobody to hear this. I guess you know that ole Simon the peddler was in the community."

"Yes," Jason replied. "He came by the house and Mom bought some flavoring and some more things."

The peddler had a horse and a cart, and he would come through the community, occasionally selling fruits, candy, flavor, medicine, and all those things. Mose went on. "Well, you know he comes to our store, and Papa buys things from him and resells them. Well, yesterday he came by, and Papa bought some things from him. The peddler was selling some blankets. He tried to get Papa to buy two of the blankets. Papa was trying to jew him down. You know Simon is a Jew don't you? Anyway, I was in the back room of Papa's store and they didn't know that I was in there."

Simon said, "Mr. Mose, if you buy three, (he lowered his voice), I'll tell you something you sho' need to know."

"What is it Simon?" Papa asked.

"You gonna buy the blanket?" Simon asked.

Papa said, "Well you tell me, and I'll let you know."

Simon lowered his voice even more. "We friends, you know. But I found out just listening that the Ku Klux Klan are going to have a meeting next week up the river, and they were

56

talking something about Crossroads. Don't tell nobody this. But you know y'all colored people and I'm a Jew. See, they don't like me either. But I heard them talking about this. And it's gonna be next Tuesday night up the river."

Mose said to Jay, "Maybe me and you can slip up there, go through the woods, and hear what's going on. You got your papa's pistol, don't you? Jay don't say nothing about this."

He continued, "I can slip Papa's pistol out of the house, and we can ride for a distance on the horses and then get out and walk the rest of the way. We can get close enough to where we can hear what's going on."

Naturally, Mose was interested in trying to find out who killed Jason's papa.

Mose said, "They don't know that I know this."

Somehow, maybe from Simon, Aunt Millipus got the news. She sent for Jay and told him that she was going to see to it that old man Koohne got the message. So Mose and Jay didn't get to go because by Monday evening they found out that there were Texas Rangers in town. That's how fast old man Koohne worked.

Jason had a chance to meet Leola at the Methodist church. She was a fine looking young woman and played the piano well. Uncle Frank's girls asked Leola if it would it be all right if Jason could sing with them—although he belonged to the Baptist church. They didn't have church on the same Sundays. That is how they got acquainted.

On Saturdays the choir rehearsed, and one day Leola said to Jason, "You have a beautiful voice, and I am glad to have you help out. People have told me a lot about you. Do you still plan on going away to school?"

"No," he said. "I will not be going. I had hoped to, but I have responsibilities of my family."

"And what did you want to be?" she asked.

"Well," he said, "I liked arithmetic and maybe I had hoped I could become a school teacher and teach mathematics and— am I saying this right?"

She laughed and said, "Of course."

She said, "I have been teaching school, and I have some books that I might even give you."

"Well," he said, "I will still need somebody to teach me."

Hesitantly, she said, "I'm living up the road there with my Uncle Frank and if you want to come to the house I'd be glad to share with you."

They were walking along the road back home, and when they had gotten to the parting place where he went right and she went left, she said, "It's been real nice talking to you, and I'm sure Uncle Frank wouldn't mind if you came up there. I'll be glad to help you anytime I can."

"That's very kind of you," he replied. "But anyway, if it's all right with Uncle Frank and his wife, I think I'll take you up on that."

And so it was that this twenty-three-year-old lady and an almost nineteen-year-old boy became friends. She helped him a lot with the books, and as time went on they spent time together, but she never talked about her past life. He only knew that she left Texas with her mother and sister years before when she was a little girl. They then moved to Nashville where she went to school to be a teacher. Her sister went to another school in Nashville to be a nurse.

So their friendship became intimate. Jay had only heard from Violet one time. He and Leola enjoyed being together— after school and at the church. He and this beautiful young lady were friends. There was something about her that attracted him even though he realized she was older, more experienced, and better educated. He felt honored that she would take the time with somebody like him.

Then one evening he went to the river to carry his fishing lines and set out his trotlines for the night. It was a balmy evening, and he loved being on the river listening to the rippling of the waters. After he had put his lines out, baited them, and put his bell on the line, he went back, and laid down on the grass on this quiet spring evening.

Somebody approaching on a horse startled him. He discovered it was Leola. She greeted him and said, "I was lonesome and just thought I would ride down the river 'cause I saw you this evening come down this way. I just needed to talk to you."

He helped her from the horse, and they stood there talking. She said, "Jay, I hope you don't think me too forward in coming down here. I have, in a way, been very lonesome, I guess, for companionship. I guess for a different kind of companion. You know that Professor at the school is a single man. He has expressed a desire that we have a courtship. But I am not the least bit interested. As a matter of fact, no man has touched me in that way since my husband died. I'm just not interested in any of these men, married or single. But Jay, there is something about you, forgive me, that does something to me. You are kind, gentle, intelligent, and if you don't mind my saying so, a very handsome young man. And somehow, I am fascinated with you. Tonight please try to understand. I just want you to put your arms around me. Let me feel the warmth of your body." There was stillness.

Jason said, "You know Leola, I guess I'm lonesome too. I told you about Violet, but she's so far away and you are here and it's hard for me to imagine you being interested in some country guy like me. And yet I feel the same way that you do. Maybe we've caught each other on the rebound. But you are a beautiful young woman. What else can I say?"

They seemed to be drawn together as if a magnet had made a contribution to this meeting. They felt themselves wrapped in each other's embrace. A lazy moon peeped over the horizon and somewhere a nightingale sang. Then they were lost in their passion for one another. The bell on the fishing line was ringing but he paid it no attention. It was as if Mother Nature was smiling on this new experience. They were lost in their affections and in that passionate relationship.

The night seemed to move faster than they wanted it to. For now the moon had turned to silver and formed shadows on the ground from the trees. And there is something about a full moon that seems to say, "this is the night for love."

Finally, she said, "I must go. Uncle Frank and Aunt Josie may be worried about me. But before I go I have to say something to you. This has been a beautiful night in my life. But if I have in any way made myself cheap in your eyes, I want to apologize, because tomorrow you may see me in a different light. If I have lost some of your respect, forgive me. But I will have to be truthful. I am not sorry. And if you don't want to see me like this again I will understand."

"Leola," he said, "to me you are somebody. And maybe it's the other way around. Maybe I took advantage of your loneliness. Maybe I'm the one that should be apologizing to you. But I have to be truthful, and I'm borrowing your same words, I cannot say that I am sorry. And if it's all right with you, I would like to see you again."

She said, "It is as you wish. Goodnight, Jay."

He stood there as she rode off into a peaceful night. He then turned and went down to the water, pulled off his clothes, and waded out to see what was ringing the bell. It was a turtle. He took his knife, cut the turtle loose, and threw it back into the water. He loved his mother's turtle soup, but tonight, well, he just wasn't going to take the turtle home. He was deeply engrossed in what had happened to him tonight.

He went home with all of this on his mind and decided he would need to talk to somebody. But who? He wondered if Leola would feel the same way come sunrise the next day. After all, she was almost five years older than he was. What would the people say about a nineteen-year-old boy going with a schoolteacher who was almost twenty-four? He knew that he was not her equal. Why would she take up time with him? So, the next evening, he went to see Mose and he said, "Come out, I need to talk to you."

They walked down the road, picked a few dewberries down the lane, and Mose finally said, "What's on your mind, man? I can see something's bothering you."

He said, "Mose, you know Leola and I have become friends. She has helped me a lot. She has been teaching me arithmetic, and other things and I like her, and she likes me. I know that I'm not her equal, but somehow we enjoy being together. What do you think?"

Mose replied, "Jay, let me tell you something. If you are going to try to please people, I can't help you. If y'all like each other and y'all become sweethearts, I ain't asking you to tell me nothing. But if y'all become sweethearts, some folks are going to say that that woman ought to be ashamed of herself going with that young boy. And if you don't, some folks are going to say that both of you are fools. Now here is a woman that has fine clothes, has a good job, is good looking and educated and you are a fool if you don't take up with her. So, look man, you're damned if you do and you're damned if you don't. Now the woman's husband is dead, so I heard, and Violet is way up there in Chicago; I don't know if she is ever coming back again. So if I was you—if y'all like each other—full steam ahead man. I sho' would like to see you be my first cousin-in-law. But I'll tell you this, my auntie that Violet is living with in Chicago is a big shot. She has this fine home and friends and I know she's going to try to marry Violet off to some city guy. And Violet might not go for it, but at the same time, what's the old saying, 'All work and no play makes Johnny a dull boy.' Man, if I was you, I'd take that woman up on that deal."

60

Jason and Leola did find time to be with each other. They were very careful because people, especially the women, talked. He respected her job. She was teaching his brothers and sisters. He kept reminding himself that she was a single lady. And she was now playing for the Methodist and Baptist churches. By the time school was out people were talking. Some said that she should have taken up with the little bald-headed professor at the school. But she resisted any of his attempts to woo her into any kind of relationship. In public, she and Jay were just good friends. But in those stolen hours they found comfort in a common feeling and yearning for the companionship that they experienced.

Then one day after school was closed Uncle Frank came to see Jay. He said, "Son, I need to talk to you. I want you to listen to me good. You probably guessed that it's about Leola and you. People are talking and they are saying that you and Leola are courting. The women are saying that Leola ought to be ashamed of herself going with a boy. Now I don't know this, and I ain't asking you any questions. But that's what the people are saying. I told Leola maybe it's best that she don't apply for jobs in the school next fall. Maybe she ought to go on to California where her sister is."

Uncle Frank continued, "I need to tell you this. Leola was raised in Nashville. When she was in college, she met a young man. I guess he was about twenty-seven or twenty-eight years old. He was a porter on a train that ran from Memphis to Nashville. His papa worked on the railroad and helped him to get this job. While he would be in Nashville, he would go to things that they would be having and on one occasion he met Leola. After awhile he asked her to marry him. He knew people in Memphis, and he would help her get a job teaching school there. She married him and moved to Memphis. She got a job teaching school. Her husband's name was Frederick Douglass—Fred was a clean, young man and popular with women. But he and Leola got along fine. Then he decided to quit the job as a porter on the train because he had to be away from home too much. He also wanted to be at home with his wife. So he got a job as a janitor in one of the tall buildings downtown. Even before they married, there were some girls and some boys who would write letters to him and her and say things that were not so nice. They would sign his name 'Fred' and sign her name as 'Leola'.

61

"Fred and Leola devised a little plan that when he wrote to her he would always sign his name 'Frederick,' never 'Fred.' That was understood. The 'F' would always be turned to the right and never to the left. The 'R' would not be joined to the 'F.' She would know that it was him who had written the letter. Likewise when she signed her name the 'L' would always be turned to the left and the 'E' would always be attached to the 'L.' In this way he would always know that it was Leola who had written the letter.

"Anyway he got a job cleaning the offices in this building, but he would have to work late after the people left.

"Now I want you to listen to me good Jay," Uncle Frank said. "In one of these offices, there was a white woman that was very friendly with Fred. Many times she would work late and would call him in to her office. She would make coffee and they would talk. It got out that this woman and Fred were going together. Now this is the talk. Anyway, one night, Fred did not come home, and the next day Leola got a letter from him saying that he was very unhappy since his father had died. The letter also said that he was also unhappy since he could not father any children because of some sickness he had when he was a little child. One of the doctors in this building told him that he would not ever be able to father any children. He was going to end it all by jumping in the Mississippi River and killing himself. But the letter was signed 'Fred.' The 'F' was turned to the left. So she did not believe that this letter was written without him being forced, and the signature 'Fred' told her something was wrong—even though it was his handwriting. There were rumors that some people say they saw him jump off the bridge. But nobody really knew. She didn't know what to do. She was hoping that in some way he was still alive. Then one late night there was a knock on her back door. She went to the door and asked who it was.

"The voice said, 'Mrs. Douglass, I am an old colored man who worked at the same building with your husband. I need to tell you something.'

"She, in the dark, opened the door and let him in.

"He said, 'I don't want you to tell nobody that I have been here. What I'm going to say I'm going to say quick and get out of here. I worked with Fred and he was a good boy. People liked him.'

"He told her about this woman that worked late and he

said, 'I heard some of the people talking in the building and they said that some white men caught him when he was leaving work. They tied his hands and tied his feet and gagged his mouth and threw him in the river. Now they say that's what happened. Fred ain't jumped in no river and drowned. But they didn't like it 'cause he was friendly with this white woman. Now don't you try to get in touch with me, please. I've got some friends that are watching and listening. If I find out anything, I'll let you know. I got to go. Goodnight.'

"About a week later, two colored men were fishing about six miles down the river and saw a body hung up in some brush. It was a colored man. His hands and feet were still tied and the gag was still around his mouth. They went and told the sheriff in that county, and the sheriff said that the body was so bad that they buried it down the river on that same day. They told those two men not say anything about it. But they got the news back to Memphis 'cause they had heard about this man.

Uncle Frank continued, "This old man went back to the house and told her what they had found out. When school was out, Leola came here to stay with me. I guess she never told you this."

"No sir, she didn't," Jay remarked.

Uncle Frank said, "So I think for her own good she needs to leave from around here and go where her sister is in California. Her momma is dead, she don't have no children, no brothers, and I don't want the people to mistreat my niece. I'm not asking you to leave her alone because I would be proud to have you as a nephew in my family. There ain't a better boy or young man in this county to me than Jason Winfield. So I'm just telling you the truth. Because of all this I think it is better for her to go to California where her sister is. I am not asking you a thing. If you decide to take my advice, that's fine. And it you decide not to, that's fine. Whatever your decision, you are still Jason Winfield in my book. I'll see you later."

Jason and Leola planned the next meeting so that they could talk. She said, "Darling, Uncle Frank told me he talked to you and told you what happened in my life. It is true. I came here torn up and lonesome, and you have filled a void in my life. I shall forever be grateful to you. I don't feel like our ages could make that much of a difference if two people are in love. I think it's how you feel. And the things that you share in common are what's important. We seem alike in so many ways. So I have de-

63

cided to go to California. I wish that I could take you with me. I would pay for the ticket and maybe we could get married and start a new life together where people are not so narrowminded. It's hard to have to go and leave you behind. Please, I don't want you to think I am bold, but I am being very honest with you. I love you Jay, and this will be a chapter in my life. It will be hard to close."

"Leola," he said, "I can't tell you in words how grateful I am to you for the precious moments we have spent together. Then you offer me a chance to see some of the world. I have never been out of the state of Texas and they say California is a wonderful place. But I can't leave my mother and my brothers and sisters. I promised my father in his dying hour that I would take care of the family. I have to do this. There is no choice for me."

"So then this is good-bye," she said.

Jay replied, "Well, maybe just for tonight I can have something to remember that this night will be both sad and happy. Let us forget about tomorrow and just think about tonight."

He reached for her and she said, "No, no, please, please. Don't put me through this again. Let's just say good-bye tonight and we will live with our memories. So this is goodnight and possibly good-bye and thanks for the memories."

Two days later she caught the train for California and another milestone was planted in the life of a boy who had lived through so much in such a short time.

Chapter 6

Good Days—Bad Days

This was a year that Jason would never forget. Events that happened would be seared in his memory. To begin with, after Leola had left, he suggested to Mose that they should give a party for the children who were going away to college. He would have a few other boys in the community make a contribution, and they would hopefully hold the party at the school building. There were five girls and four boys; three were the Washington brothers who lived at the end of Dogwood Lane. They would be going to various colleges—three of them would be attending colleges out of the state and six would be going to colleges in the state. The school had what is known as subtrustees who were three colored men of the community. These subtrustees received their orders from the white trustees who were over the entire district. Both the Negro school and the white school were in the district. The subtrustees gave them permission to have the party.

Jason and Mose moved the benches in the school and borrowed tables to put in one room where they would serve tea-cakes and lemonade. In the new room of the school they moved the benches out and put chairs around the wall. They left the piano in and made room for those who wanted to dance. They secured the service of a man in the community, Buck Jones, who played the piano, guitar, and banjo. He drifted into this community . . . some people say from one of the old states. But he could really play music. He was living with a young woman in her late twenties, named Clara Bell Mays, who was a niece of Uncle Sam Moore. She was a very attractive young woman, and some men said she walked like a proverbial showhorse. Many of the men found her to be a good-looking lady, but Buck Jones was very jealous of her. He took good care of her. She had good clothes and jewelry but very few associates. He kept money on hand because he had roosters that he would take to fight other roosters. He also had greyhounds that he would run and bet on. They also said that he operated dice games. But he could really play music. So he played the piano for the dance. People were a little surprised that he brought Clara Bell with him, but then they said he was scared of leaving her at home because everybody knew where he was.

It was a gala affair. Some of the young girls cut paper and decorated the building. They put on their best dresses, and you would have thought that you were at some affair in a big city. During the dance some young men from the Red Bluff community asked Clara Bell to dance with them. When Buck saw them dancing together, he stopped playing the piano and everybody knew he was upset. He went over to where they were and said something to the guy, who pushed him back. Clara Bell tried to settle the argument without creating an embarrassing situation. He told her to shut up. The guy said something to Buck, which infuriated him. By that time Buck made a lunge at him, and Jason ran up and got between them and pleaded, "Don't do that fellows."

Buck swung at the man, and Jason tried to prevent it. He hit Jason and made a knot on his head. They finally got it settled. But he was heard to tell Clara Bell, "I'll get you when we get home." That was Friday night.

Jason and Mose agreed to meet at the school at one o'clock on Saturday afternoon to put everything back in place. Jason, as usual, was a little early and Mose, as usual, was a little late.

By the time Mose arrived, Uncle Sam rode up on his horse. He was furious. He lost no time in jumping all over Jason with his talk. He had heard what had happened the night before. Evidently, the way he had heard it was that Jason and Buck had a fight over Clara Bell.

Mose shook his head and said, "Man, I'm sorry. I intended to tell you this before he got here."

Anyway, Uncle Sam blasted him for using the school to have a dance. He said, "That was not what the school was for. It was for learning the students. You was the one who went to the subtrustees to get permission and then you go and have a fight with Buck Jones."

Uncle Sam continued, "And it would look like you would stop somewhere . . . you just run Leola out of town. That gal could have had her job teaching right now if you hadn't run her down and disgraced her and her family. And she ain't been gone long enough for her tracks to be blowed out by the wind before you right here trying to go with my niece. And you know she was Buck Jones' sweetheart. But to me, look like you like old women. It's a shame."

Uncle Sam said, "When I leave here I'm going to Koohne Town and report this to the white school trustees. I'm going to put it in their hands. I know it's true, 'cause Clara Bell came to my house this morning and she had whelps on her where Buck had beat her up. And you the cause of it. I got a letter right here in my jumper pocket that I wrote to my sister in Chicago."

Mose shook his head and said under his breath to Jason, "He can't write. One of the girls wrote that letter. I'll tell you about it."

Uncle Sam continued. "I'm going to mail this letter today and I told my sister-in-law to let Violet read the letter about what all happened and how you been running women down here . . . and somebody said you were going to California following Leola . . . and now you trying to go with Clara Bell and trying to get her killed . . . and I told her that I didn't want Violet to come back here no more 'cause Jason Winfield is nothing but a black skunk. That's what I think about you."

He turned and rode off on his old gray nag, and Mose shook his head and said again, "Man, I'm sorry."

"Now let me tell you what really happened," Mose said. "You know Buck is crazy about Clara Bell, and she is afraid of him. She can't go to but about two houses in this community, and that's Uncle Sam's house and our house. He won't even allow her to go to the store unless she rides with Uncle Sam or somebody like that. And the few times that she went to church, he accused her of going with the deacon, not papa now, but one or two of the others. And he even said that Parson Prince liked her. Man, this man is crazy. But he can sho' play a piano. I give it to him. Anyway after he left home this morning, Clara Bell walked down to Uncle Sam and Aunt Clara's house to talk to Aunt Clara. She told her what had happened and that she was going to run away from Buck the first chance she got. I don't have to tell you not to say anything about this. Uncle Sam got it all backward. He thought that when Buck hit you on the head that y'all were fighting. But that's Uncle Sam."

So Jay figured that when Violet got this letter, it would be the end of everything for him.

Two weeks later Jason heard a knock on his door about 3 o'clock in the morning. It was Mose. Jason opened the door and let Mose in. His clothes were wet because it had been raining.

Jason said, "Man, where you come from in this weather?"

Mose said, "I'll tell you, but first get me some dry clothes." They could wear each other's clothes.

Jason got him some dry clothes and said, "Come on in the kitchen. We can talk."

They sat down and Mose spoke softly. "I have just come back from Red Bluff."

"What were you doing in Red Bluff?" Jason asked.

"Listen, man," he said softly, "Clara Bell has run off from Buck Jones."

"And what's that got to do with you going to Red Bluff?" Jason asked.

"I took her on my horse," Mose said.

"What?" Jason asked.

Mose continued, "Let me get through telling you. She is on her way to the territory, you know that's Oklahoma. That's where they say they are giving land away."

"And how did you wind up taking her, Mose?" Jason continued to question.

"Man," Mose said, "you ain't going to believe this. I was over at Uncle Sam's yesterday, and Clara Bell was there. She asked me to do her favor. And I said yes—if I could. She said, 'I'll give you two dollars if you'll do it.' I asked her what did she want me to do. She told me that she wanted me to come to her house tonight, close to ten o'clock, and tie the horse in the pasture away from the house. I was then to go out behind the smokehouse and stay there until she would turn off the lamplight in her window.

"She said, 'When I turn the light out, I want you to run up on the porch and knock loudly. I'll ask who it is, and you should say 'It's me.' If you do that I'll give you the two dollars. I'll give you one now and the other tonight.'"

Mose said, "That's all she told me. I got the two dollars. Tonight about ten o'clock I was out there behind this house and I was wondering what was going on. I don't know if I dozed off or what, but if I did it must have only been for a minute or two. When I looked up the light was out in the window, and I jumped up and ran through the yard and ran up on the porch and knocked on the door just like she told me.

"That's what I did. When she asked who it was I said in a gruff voice, 'It's me.' And she said, 'Just a minute' and she opened the door.

"She said, 'Go get the horse real quickly. I'm getting ready to run off from Buck. Go get the suitcases. I'm getting ready to go to Aunt Millipus' house.'

"When we went to Aunt Millipus' house she told me to put her suitcase under the porch and she said, 'Come on and go with me Mose.'

"She knocked on the door and Aunt Millipus said, 'Who knocked?' Clara Bell said, 'This is Clara Bell, I need to talk to you.'

"Aunt Millipus opened the door and said, 'Girl, where you going this time of night? And Mose where you going?'

"She said, 'Aunt Millipus I need your help. I need it bad. I'm running away from Buck. 'Cause he's going to kill me. I want you to please help me, please help me Aunt Millipus.'

"'And what do you want me to do?' Aunt Millipus asked.

"Clara Bell said, 'I want you to give me a lucky hand. I'm trying to get to the territory, and I need some luck.'

"Aunt Millipus looked at her and said, 'Clara, I can't make you a lucky hand. I don't know why the people think I can. I tried to learn that years ago in Louisiana, but that's behind me now. I'm a Christian. I believe in the Lord and all I can do is pray for you. I don't mind doing that, but I can't give you a lucky hand.'

"Clara Bell didn't seem to be listening. She kept pleading. 'Please Aunt Millipus, Help me. Give me a lucky hand.'

"Aunt Millipus said, 'Let's pray.' Then Aunt Millipus got down on her knees and she must have talked to the Lord.

"Then I said, 'If the Lord don't hear this woman tonight, he must be somewhere out of pocket.'

"But Clara Bell was still not satisfied. So she said, 'Aunt

Millie I know something that you sho' want to know. And if you help me, I'll tell you what it is. You really want to know this.'

"'What is it Clara Bell?' she asked.

"'Just give me something lucky and I'll tell you something you really want to know,' Clara Bell said.

"Aunt Millipus got up, went over to her trunk, and took some keys from around her neck. She unlocked the trunk and looked down in there and came out with a rabbit foot.

"She said, 'Clara Bell, a fortune teller gave me this rabbit foot nearly twenty years ago for my luck. Since I know the Lord now, I don't need it no more. So tell me what this big secret is and I'll give you my lucky rabbit foot.'

"Clara Bell said, 'I got to hurry Aunt Millie. But you know Clyde Black, that white man that lives on down the road. He been mettling me and wanting me to go with him behind Buck's back. I told him two or three times I wasn't interested in no white man. But yesterday he came by my house and showed me a ten-dollar bill and told me if I would go to bed with him that he would give me that ten-dollar bill. I told him no. Then he pulled a five dollar bill out and said he would make it $15 if I would let him come by when Buck was gone.'

"She continued, 'Then the thought hit me. With $15 I could buy a ticket to the territory. So I decided to trick him. I told him to come back that night about ten o'clock 'cause Buck would be gone with the rooster fighting or playing for somebody. And I told him to walk 'cause I didn't want Buck to come back and find a horse around the place. What I planned to do was to make him give me the money, and then I would get Mose to be outside and when I put the lamp out, Mose would come up on the porch after I get the money. That way I would tell him that it was Buck. I would have the money and he would have to run out. So Buck came and knocked on my door, and I let him in.'

"I listened tentatively as she continued the story. 'The moment he got in the house he grabbed me, and I said, 'Wait Clyde don't be so fast.' He didn't seem to be able to wait and I was struggling with him. I said, 'Give me the money first,' and he gave me the $15. He was almost like a tiger. I said, 'Wait, you don't have to be in such a hurry.' He was almost slinging me on the bed, and I was desperately trying to get to the lamp so Mose would come on. When I got close enough to the lamp, I blew it out and balled the money up in my hand in the dark. By that time he had his shirt off and he was climbing all over me like a tiger.'

"Clara Bell looked straight at Aunt Millipus as she went one. 'Aunt Millipus, here's the part I want to tell you. You remember the night that they killed Wade at the school closing? Well, one of those Ku Klux Klan people stood right over me and he had a strong odor from his body. Aunt Millipus, I swear tonight when he was wrestling with me I smelt that same odor. Clyde Black was one of the Ku Klux Klan men in that bunch that killed Wade Winfield.'

"Her voice quickened as she continued to speak. She said, 'Anyway, I was hoping and praying for Mose to come on and then suddenly I heard footsteps on the porch and a knock on the door and I said to Clyde, 'Get out of here real quick. That's Buck and he'll kill both of us.'

"She said that Clyde jumped up and grabbed his shirt and ran out of the back door barefoot because he left his boots. She said, 'Aunt Millipus this is the truth. I wouldn't be with that fellow for $115, and I know he's going to be mad. So now you know all I've been saying is that Clyde Black is a member of the Ku Klux Klan.'

"Aunt Millie gave Clara Bell that rabbit foot and said, 'God bless you honey.'

Mose said, "And she gave me two more dollars to take her to Red Bluff to put her on that train. I ran into that shower of rain on my way back. But I'm not going to stay with you the rest of the night. I'm going home 'cause if I did stay and people found out that Clara Bell ran off, they are going to say that you had something to do with it."

Jay was saddened 'cause it brought back painful memories. Whether it was Clyde who pulled the trigger, he guess he would never know. But that question would remain in his mind.

Because there was no advance weather information, they did not know that there was a hurricane in the Gulf of Mexico and the 30 mph winds and showers of rain were a result of the approach of the hurricane in East Texas which was travelling northeast. It rained all day. As a matter of fact it rained for about three days. There was a big flood on the river. The water was so high that people had to come out of the bottom and stay with relatives. Some stayed at the schoolhouse, others stayed at churches. It was the worst flood they had witnessed. Houses were washed away. Cattle were floating downstream. People were trying to get their cattle to higher ground, and Clyde and Claude rode horses with other men across creeks. Clyde's horse swam for awhile then laid on one side, and Clyde was drowned in the flood.

It was a bad time, and there were people who said that Aunt Millipus put a hex on Clyde. Aunt Millipus only said that the Lord would take care of that situation. And that he did.

The September flood didn't get to Jason's property because it was near the creeks and not in the bottoms. He made a bumper crop that year. His cotton was head high, and the rain came just in time to fill the cotton bolls out. He made so much corn that he realized he would have to build a larger barn. So he tore the old barn down, and one evening while he was out there removing old hay that was on the ground inside the barn, the eye hoe he was using struck something under the hay. Lo and behold it was the crock that his father had hidden that held ten twenty-dollar gold pieces. He gently lifted the crock out and in the semi-darkness counted the coins. Sure enough there were ten twenty-dollar gold coins.

The very first thing that he thought about was taking the money somewhere to show the people that his father hadn't been a cattle wrestler. This would also clear his father's record about where the money came from.

As he went into the house where his mother was he thought, "What a year this has been."

She said, "Jay you keep the money. You're running the farm. You did what you think is best. I got my buggy. I got my horse. So you take the money. I know you're going to do what's right."

That is when the idea came to him that he would do something that he hoped to do sometime in the future. There was a man whose land adjoined his. The man wanted to sell his land. It was about seventy acres of timber pine trees on the land. He had often thought that one day he would like to buy that land and cut down the pine trees and sell them. After talking with his mother he went to Koohne Town with her consent to try to borrow money from old man Koohne's bank. He would take this money and some of the money that he had made from his crop and use it as a deposit and borrow the rest from the bank. This is something he had never done before. When he walked into the bank, one of the teller's asked, "What can I do for you?"

There were two windows at the bank. He said, "I'd like to talk to Mr. Koohne."

The teller went into another room and presently came back. He said, "Mr. Koohne will see you. Go in."

Old man Koohne said, "Good morning, Jason. How are you doing?"

"Fine, thank you, Mr. Koohne," replied Jason.

"Sit down," said Mr. Koohne. "What can I do for you?"

Jason told him why he was there.

Old man Koohne leaned back in his chair, folded his arms, and said, "Jason, they tell me you made a good crop, and I like to see young men, black or white, try to do something for themselves. I have to say, it took a lot of courage for you to come here and want me to loan you some money to buy some land. But your papa was a good man. And I guess you got some of that after him. But Jay, you know business is business. How much did you say you wanted to borrow?"

Jason said, "One thousand dollars."

Mr. Koohne said, "Jason, do you know what the word collateral means."

"Yes sir, I do think I know what that means. It means to put up something of yours, to make a lien," Jason answered.

"If I loan you a thousand dollars, Jason, what do you have to put up?" Mr. Koohne asked.

Jason said, "I have $500 cash. I talked with my momma, and we have twenty acres of land that papa bought—not the home part—and she's willing to borrow money against that twenty acres. We'll put the $500 down, and if we don't pay you in the time allotted, you get the seventy acres of land."

Old man Koohne stood up and said, "I think I'm going to take you up on that Jason. I don't need any more land. I will help you. If you don't pay it, then the land will be mine. Remember, always do business as business should be done. Now go and talk with that man and go and talk with your momma and y'all come back here. If everything is in order, I'll let you have the one thousand dollars for the land."

Jason did buy the land. The deal went through. School didn't open until the middle of October so that the children could pick cotton. This meant that the school closed the middle of April instead of the first of the month since school was held just for six months.

It was during the middle of harvest time when Jay received a letter from Violet. The very next week he received a letter from Leola. Violet's letter said she was hurt by what she heard he had been doing. It was hard for her to believe, but a friend had already written her about Leola. She said she would just probably not come back because she was heartbroken. He had betrayed her trust, and she never would have believed that this would happen.

Leola's letter was different. It wasn't a long letter. She just said that she liked the climate there in California and that her sisters were glad to see her. She said she would have a hard time forgetting him because of the type of person he was.

She said in closing:

> I guess you are a little different than any man that I have met and there will always be a warm place in my heart for you. I hope I have not spoiled your life but I have to confess, if I had to do it again I would probably do the same thing. If you ever need me or if you decide to come to California, let me know and I will send you a ticket.
>
> As always,
> Leola

It was the last week in the year—just two days past Christmas, and one of the things that Jay was mindful of was that women did not wash clothes between Christmas and New Year's because they said it was bad luck. He was glad this year, because it was awfully cold that morning.

As he prepared to go and help the Randolph's kill hogs, he reflected on the events that had happened—especially those which had occurred during this particular year. He remembered that his mother had finally stopped wearing a black dress and a black veil to church every Sunday. She had done this since his father had been dead over a year. That was a practice among widows who lost their husbands—they had to mourn for a year. Her wearing black always reminded him of his father's death.

He reflected on how much help Leola had been to him with studying math and English—two of his favorite subjects. He could not easily forget his relationship with her. He allowed himself just for a moment to think about Uncle Sam and how he had chewed him out about the party at the school and accused him of liking older women. He remembered Uncle Sam muttering something as he rode off that day. Mose had said that Uncle Sam said, "I wouldn't put it by him. He was probably going with old lady Millipus." He wondered how low a person's mind could get.

He remembered Clara Bell running away from Buck Jones

and Uncle Sam accusing him of being the cause. Clara Bell had only written two people since she had been gone. She had written a letter to Aunt Millipus thanking her for what she had done. She also had written a short letter to Mose and put it in the envelope that she sent to Aunt Millipus. Mose said she told Aunt Millipus that if she ever came back to Texas, she would have a husband. But at the time she was living in a town called Langston, Oklahoma, which only had black people living there. She had found a job working at the Colored Agricultural and Normal University that was later known as Langston University.

Jason remembered how Buck had gone through the community asking questions to try to find out where Clara Bell had gone. However, only Mose, Aunt Millipus, and he knew where she was.

He remembered the flood and Clyde Black being drowned. There had been talk that Chester Winfield, who had finished law school and had joined a firm in a town that was about fifty miles away, had been secretly working on Wade Winfield's death. He was trying to find out who the klansmen were. The talk was that Chester had gotten enough information and had been given the names of the klansmen. He was going to turn state evidence. He also had heard that Clyde had not drowned but that one of the klansmen killed him to keep him silent. Clyde's brother Claude never really got over it. Christmas Eve night he had been drinking, drew a gun on a fellow at a saloon, and the man beat him to the draw and killed him. But the talk was that since Claude was going to name the other klansman; he had been set up.

Jason hoped that as the curtain came down on this year, nothing else would happen, because truly there had been good days and bad days.

Chapter 7

Victoria Finds Out Who She Is from Aunt Millipus

With the butcher knives that he had sharpened on the previous evening on his grinding stone, Jay walked briskly up the road that morning in the cold northern to help Deacon Winfield and his family kill hogs. It was a big thing when two or three families got together and helped each other at hog killing time. He had seen Uncle Frank ride by earlier on his horse. He would also be helping with the hog killing. This meant that there would be bacon, ham, jowl, pickled pig's feet, chitlings, and cracklins by the end of the day. There would also be cans of lard. People always said that there was not a man between East Texas and El Paso who could trim a ham like Uncle Frank Cotton.

As he walked alone he saw smoke coming out of Aunt Millipus' chimney and also out of the stovepipe in her kitchen. He knew she must have been fixing breakfast, which he thought was a bit early for her, since she had been having rheumatism. Then he discovered why. Galloping along in the wind on a horse was Victoria Webb going to Aunt Millipus' house.

Even before he got to the Randolph's house he could see the fire burning around two black wash pots and heating the water to scald the hogs once they were killed. Yet he wondered what brought Victoria to Aunt Millipus so early in the morning.

She would occasionally go down to have dinner in the evening, so it was not too unusual. He had noticed that she had a package in her gloved hands, which he assumed was probably a Christmas present.

Jason was right. Victoria did come to have breakfast with Aunt Millipus, who had invited her because she wanted to talk with her. Aunt Millipus opened the door and said, "Oh, come on in honey. I thought it might be too cold for you. It's really cold out there."

"Oh," Victoria said, "I made it just fine." She continued, "Everything smells so good already. I think I'll eat like a pig. Oh I brought you a Christmas present. I'm sorry that I didn't give it to you Christmas day. But I have been running ever since I got in from school and, Trey—you know old man Richard Koohne's grandson—has been carrying me so fast every since I've been back. He just does not want me out of his sight. But really he's a jewel. And his grandparents, they are already calling me their granddaughter. Anyway, here I am, and here is your present." She hugged Aunt Millipus and kissed her on the cheek. "Merry Christmas," she said.

"Thank you," Aunt Millipus said. "I've got you a present, but we're going to eat first. Then I'll look at mine and you can look at yours," she said.

They ate their breakfast and Aunt Millipus said to just leave everything in the kitchen like it was. She said, "I've got all day to wash my dishes."

But Victoria said, "Aunt Millipus, I don't mind helping you."

"No," Aunt Millipus said, "I'll do it. This old rheumatism bothers me, and when I feel better I'll wash my dishes. Come on now let's go into my bedroom. I want to talk to you."

Aunt Millipus motioned for Victoria to sit down. They sat in the two rocking chairs in front of the fireplace in her bedroom. The fire was glowing in the fireplace. A big oak backlog had been in there since yesterday when Jason had come over and put it in the fireplace. He also had stacked wood on her porch and in a box by the fireplace. The house was warm and very comfortable.

"Now I'm fine," Victoria said. "What did you want to talk about? I'm anxious to hear. Is it good or bad?" she asked.

"Well," Aunt Milipus said, "I guess some of both. Anyway, it's how you look at it."

"What is it?" Victoria said. "I'm anxious to hear this. You have always been frank with me. Did I do something wrong? Is it something about me?" She rattled off the questions.

"No," she said, "it's about me."

"Well, I'm all ears, Aunt Millipus, tell me." With that statement Victoria prepared herself to hear what Aunt Millipus had to say.

Aunt Millipus sat back in her chair, folded her arms across her chest, and closed her eyes for a moment. She began with the story of her life in Jackson Quarters. She told about her mother, her own childhood, and her relationship with Colonel George's son. She also told about her two children by George Jr. Victoria sat quietly and listened.

Aunt Millipus said, "Do you want me to go on?"

Victoria said, "Yes, please go on, by all means."

Aunt Millipus said, "You looked at me so funny while I was telling the story. I'm just telling you the truth. You have to believe me. This is what happened."

"I believe you Aunt Millipus," she said. "It's just that I never realized you had been through anything like this. Please go on."

She told her about her two children, Johnie and Jeannie Mae. She told her about Harvey, the young black man with whom she fell in love. She told her about what had happened on that night when Colonel George caught her and Harvey and how they became separated and never saw him again. She told her about the death of George and told her in detail about the deeds and the money in that black bag in the trunk in the attic.

Aunt Millipus told her about George's brother-in-law, Jeff Reynolds, coming to Jackson Quarters to operate the plantation for his sister. And she told her about her son who was retarded. She also told her about how Jeff Reynolds later raped her fifteen-year-old daughter, Jeannie Mae. She told her about the fight between Jeff and her son—Johnie was not to be forgotten. Johnie fled from the plantation and she and her daughter left the same night to go to New Orleans. She explained how hurt she felt a few weeks later when she realized that Jeff Reynolds had impregnated her daughter. The birth of the baby and her daughter's thoughts that she, Aunt Millipus, didn't like the baby because she looked white was also memorable. Her grandbaby was so light that you could not tell her from any white child in New Orleans.

Victoria listened attentively as Aunt Millipus went on to relate how Jeannie Mae had left without her knowing where she went. She was not able to find her. She had neither seen nor heard from her until a year and a half later when she came homesick without the little baby. She told Victoria how disappointed she was about Jeannie Mae not bringing the baby back with her.

"But she told me," Aunt Millipus went on, "about her marriage to a man in Lake Charles, about the man dying, and about her going to San Antonio for health reasons. She found out that she had tuberculosis. Jeannie Mae left the child with a white couple who had befriended her on the train. She had found out the name of this couple and where they were going and then a few days later Jeannie Mae died.

"After Jeannie Mae's death, I was left with no relatives because she had never heard from her son who had run off at the age of seventeen. The only living relative who I had was Jeannie Mae's baby, and she didn't know where the baby was. After some months she wanted to find this child so badly that she left New Orleans and came to Texas to look for the baby."

She paused and there was quietness in the room. Then she said, "And Victoria, you are that child."

Victoria's hand was on the arms of the chair and her white knuckles were seemingly protruding from her hands as if she was having a problem believing what she was hearing.

Aunt Millipus went on. "You are my grandchild. The only relative that I know that I have in this world. Let me show you something," she said.

She got up out of the chair walked over to where Victoria was. "Excuse me," she said.

She pulled up her own apron and dress to her waist, pulled down her flannel underwear, and said, "Look, you see this tattoo on my thigh? When you were a baby I had a woman put a tattoo on your thigh. I asked at that time if it was going to hurt. I didn't want it to hurt you, but if it did I wanted to hurt with you. Please forgive me. I did it because this way if anyone would take you away from us, since you looked white, I would have a way to find you."

Aunt Millipus continued, "So when I came to Koohne Town I was looking for a couple with the name of Webb who had a little girl who was going on three years old. I managed to get a job working for them and could hardly wait to see if there was a tattoo on your body. So when I bathed you, there it was. And Victoria, that's what I wanted to tell you. It's true, all of this is true. You are my grandchild."

Victoria got up and walked over to the window. She stood with her back to Aunt Millipus as she looked out on a cold bleak December day. A few blowing snowflakes were now falling on an evergreen Cyprus bush in Aunt Millipus' yard and seemed almost as if they were pronouncing a death nell to her once contented life.

She said, "When I was a little girl, I remember one time I asked my momma why this 'x' was on my thigh. She told me that during the war there were a lot of misplaced people and separation of families and that people began to put tattoos on their babies in order to find them in case they became lost. Why did you wait so long to tell me?"

"Well," Aunt Millipus replied, "I guess I wanted to see you happy and have a good life. But now that I have gotten old and sick and rheumatism is getting me down, I don't feel that I have much longer to live.

With her back still to Aunt Millipus, Victoria said, "They tell me no one ever dies of arthritis."

"Arthritis?" Aunt Millipus asked.

"Yes," Victoria replied, "It's another name for rheumatism."

"Well that may be so," Aunt Milipus said, "but when you have it like I have, sometimes you think you are going to die."

Aunt Millipus continued, "But anyway, my heart flutters at times. Something is wrong with my heart and when I walk a long way I can hardly get my breath. So I know something is wrong with my heart.

"Everybody dies with something, Victoria, and since I feel like I don't have much longer to live, I want to make out my will. Since you are the only relative I have, I want to leave everything to you including that two hundred acres of land. That is, if you will accept it," Aunt Millipus said.

Victoria turned, faced Aunt Millipus, and ran both of her hands through her own hair, and said, "Aunt Millipus I am shocked. What else can I say?" Then she sat down in her chair and put her head in her hands.

Aunt Millipus said, "I think you are having a hard time believing what I am telling you, but I want to show you something."

80

She took her key from around her neck, unlocked her trunk and came out with a black bag. The first thing that she brought out was a Bible.

She handed it to Victoria and said, "My momma gave me this Bible before she died. And if you will look in the front part, I have when my momma died—I wrote it in the Bible—I wrote in there, when Johnie was born—you turn to it, it's there, when Jeannie Mae was born. It shows when George Jr. died, and when you were born. We named you Queen Victoria. You see it in that book? Your birthday. In that book is when your momma Jeannie Mae Jackson died and where."

Victoria sat there reading these entries. Aunt Millipus went back into her bag. "Here are the deeds for 200 acres of land that your grandfather left for you, Johnie, Jeannie Mae, and me. You look at it. Here are your momma's engagement and wedding rings. Here is a necklace that her husband gave her before she died. Look at it, there are two little diamonds in it.

"Here is the paper that I got from the courthouse in New Orleans when you were born. The midwife turned it in and I went up there and got a copy of it. All I have to say is, I know this has to be a shock to you, but whatever you decide that is what I will do. There are only two people in the whole state of Texas that I've told this to, and they swore to me that they will never tell. Those two people are Professor Love and Jason Winfield. This beautiful necklace is what I wanted to give you for a Christmas present." Aunt Millipus ended her story.

When Jay looked over to Aunt Millipus' house, he saw Victoria riding away. At first she was galloping, but now she had the horse trotting as she rode home.

His mother had come over in the buggy to help Miss Elizabeth (she didn't allow people to call her auntie) to fix dinner for the men. She also helped to grind the meat into sausages and to cook the fat into lard. As they watched her go into the house to eat, he looked and there was only a little smoke coming out of Aunt Millipus' chimney. He wondered if Aunt Millipus had finally told Victoria the whole truth.

The women had to cook liver, backbones, ribs, dewberry cobbler, sweet potato pon, and everything else that they could think about. Then all the men and the boys sat at the table and ate.

Late that evening Jay and his mother finally went home in the buggy. From the work with the neighbors they carried a small sack of meat because that's how they did it when neighbors killed hogs. They always exchanged meat.

Old man Mose had asked them to drop off some meat for Aunt Millipus. Miss Lizzy had told them to tell Aunt Millipus that the reason they didn't send for her to help as usual was because it was cold, and they thought it would be hard on her rheumatism.

Getting her stick, she walked out on the porch and waved with her right hand to Cindy and asked, "You want to get out?"

"No," she answered. "We got to go see about the child. How are you feeling?" Cindy asked.

"Oh, fairly well," Aunt Millipus replied. She thanked Jay for the meat and leaning on her cane walked back in the house.

Jason and his mother went on home.

The new year was somewhat uneventful. Jay just dedicated himself to his job. He had hired a couple of men to help him cut down trees and had a contract with a lumberyard, which bought the trees to make lumber. He still was trapping animals and selling hides and occasionally working for Mrs. Winfield. As a result he was able to save enough money to pay the note at the bank. He had also sold some yearlings from the momma cows and had applied that to the loan.

The first part of May, Aunt Clara Moore had a stroke and she was now bedridden. She kept crying because she wanted to see her baby Violet. She worried them so much until they wrote to Violet and her Aunt Dora, her mother's sister, to tell them that Aunt Clara wanted to see her baby child.

That is when, to his surprise, Jason received a letter from Violet. It was very brief. It said that she was looking forward to coming home and seeing all of her friends again. She said she guessed it would be between two or three weeks, and she had plans to stay for about two weeks. She said that she heard that Jay was very busy these days and that she was happy for him. She wanted Jay to tell all the gang that she would see them no later than the first of June.

He read the letter over and over. There was no hint of how she felt or didn't feel about him. He wondered why she would write him. Anyway, he put the letter in one of his drawers where he kept his papers and went back to the business of trying to make a living.

Violet and her Aunt Dora came the first part of June. It was coincidental that on Saturday morning Jay and one of the men he worked with had gone to Koohne Town to pick up some supplies in the wagon. As they rode down the main street, his driver had mules trotting as they were in a hurry to get back to the work. As he passed one of the grocery stores, he saw two ladies in the store at the counter. He looked back at these two ladies who had come out on the board sidewalk with bags in their hands.

He told his driver to stop and shouted, "Stop man, that's Violet." He jumped out of the wagon, and at the same time Violet looked up and recognized him from a distance. He started running toward her on the street. She set her paper bag down and was running to meet him. When they met up they embraced each other. She said, "Oh, Jay, I'm so glad to see you."

He said, "You are not half as glad as I am." People came out of the store to watch them. The couple was unaware of the people watching them. Her sister explained that they were coming to town to get their mother some supplies and were getting ready to go home in the buggy.

"We just arrived last night and I had no idea that I would see you here this morning," Violet said.

He picked up her groceries and they walked back to her buggy. He helped her in and said, "Violet, I'm really happy to see you again. I want you to know that there is not one doubt in my mind that I feel just like I did that evening at the school closing. I hope that there is even a spark in your heart for me. Please don't let it go out."

She said, "Jay, I feel the same way, but we need to talk because there are some things that need to be cleared up. Once that is done . . . well, we'll see what happens. You need to tell me some things."

Naturally, Mose had it all figured out. He knew that Uncle Sam didn't want Jay at his house. He talked his momma into asking Violet to have dinner with them. They could ask her the next day after church. She knew Aunt Dora would not be going and would be at home with Aunt Clara. This would let Jay and Violet have a chance to talk. Miss Lizzy was for it because she didn't like Uncle Sam either. So the next day, which was Sunday, Deacon Randolph and Miss Lizzy sat out on the porch, the girls took a nap, and Mose went over to unlock the store to get something out of it.

They let Jay and Violet talk in the sitting room. She questioned him about Leola and he said, "Violet, I want you to understand something. Leola helped me with some studies, which is now paying off for me in my little business. We were together a lot and I was lonesome. I was not hearing from you my friendship with Leola kind of got out of hand. She too was lonesome, she had lost her husband, and I guess we found consolation in each other. That's how it was.

"I'm sorry if this offended you, but the moment I saw you again I realized I could never love another person. I still want you to be my wife. Will you? Do I have to get on my knees? I'm ready to do it," he said.

"Jason Winfield," she said, "I guess I looked real silly yesterday running down the street to meet you, and then when we embraced publicly. I think my actions answer your question. Whatever you did I forgive you. I still want to be Mrs. Jason Winfield one of these days."

"Well then," he said, "why don't we go get married. We need each other. You don't have to go back."

"I can't right now," she said. "You see, Aunt Dora's husband is sick, and I have been helping her with him. His sister is staying there at the house with him while we are here. I promised her that I would come back and help her with her husband and finish my schooling. I just have one more year then I'll be graduating from college."

"And you'll come home when you graduate and we'll get married?" Jason said.

"Yes," she replied.

"That's a promise?" he asked.

"Yes, Jay, that's a promise," she remarked.

Aunt Dora had a special delivery after a week, saying her husband had taken worse and she needed to go home right away. They decided that Aunt Dora would go back immediately, but that Violet would stay on another week with her mother. Jason only saw her briefly with the help of Mose. Mose took pleasure in outfoxing Uncle Sam who was determined to keep Jason and Violet apart.

When her week was up, Violet got ready to catch the train back to Chicago. On the day that she was to leave, Jason went to Mose's house. He had been to Koohne's Town and he was all cleaned up. He said to Mose, "I want you to do something for me."

Mose in his usual demeanor said, "Name it partner. I'll do it if I can."

84

"You can," Jason said.

"Don't keep me guessing. What do you want me to do for you?" Mose said.

"I want you to go with me Mose," Jason said. "I'm going to the next town beyond Koohne Town on my horse. I want you to ride with me."

"And what are you going to do up there?" Mose asked.

Jason replied, "I am going to catch that train that Violet will be on, and I am going on to the city, and I am going to marry Violet."

"You're what? Man are you going crazy?" Mose exclaimed.

"No," Jay replied.

He reached into his pocket and pulled out a brown envelope and handed it to Mose.

He said he had just come from the courthouse and got his marriage license.

Jay repeated himself, "I'm going to catch that train, and Violet and I are going to get off in the next city and get married."

"Have ya'll talked about this?" Mose asked.

"No," Jay admitted.

"What do you mean? How are you going to do something like this? What about her going to Chicago? Are you going to Chicago?" Mose asked many questions.

"No," Jay replied calmly. "I'm going to let her go on to Chicago. I want you to meet me at Red Bluff tomorrow when I come back."

"All right, if that's what you want. Man, I don't understand you sometimes. You are going to let your wife—if she marries you—go on to Chicago and you will be down here in Texas?" Mose asked quizzically.

"That's my plan," Jay said.

Jason was waiting when the train pulled into the station, and he walked into the colored section. He spotted Violet with her back to him and he walked up to the aisle to the seat where she was sitting alone.

When she looked up, she almost screamed, "Jay, where in the world did you come from? Oh Lord."

They again embraced each other. People were looking, and she said, "Where are you going?"

"Sit down," he said. "I came to marry you. Can we get married?"

"Married? Jay what do you mean?" Violet asked.

"I bought the license this morning. When we get to the city you already told me you wanted to get married. I want to marry you tonight," Jay said.

"And then what will happen?" Violet asked.

"Tomorrow I will put you on the train and let you go to Chicago. But I want you to be my wife when you leave Texas. I've got the license and surely you won't turn me down," Jay said.

They got off the train in the city and the black man at the station told them where a preacher lived. He paid this man to carry them to the preacher's house so that they could get married. The preacher was happy to do it. His wife consented to be the witness.

He looked at Jason and said to his wife, "My, she is a pretty girl. Don't you think so honey?"

He wife said, "Honey don't you think he is handsome? They make a beautiful couple."

When Jay and Violet explained their situation, the preacher's wife said, "We will have to give you some cake." They also got some grape juice.

Jason asked if they had a room where they could spend the night. The pastor said that he had a member of his church who had a house that was vacant. It was located three doors down. He assured them that since school was out and the teachers were not living there now that the owner would certainly allow them to stay for the night.

The pastor carried them down to the house and introduced them to the lady. He explained that they had just gotten married and needed a place to stay for the night. The lady was overjoyed for them to stay, and when she found out the situation she told them that she would not charge them anything. It would be her wedding present to them.

It was a nice little apartment. There was a bedroom, a small sitting room, and a kitchen. The lady put fresh linens on the bed and tidied up the room.

"Since this is your first night of marriage, I'm going to light some candles for y'all," she said.

The pastor said goodnight to them. He also offered to take them to the train station in the morning. He turned to the lady and asked, "Don't you think they are a beautiful couple?"

"Oh yes, beautiful," she said. Speaking to the couple she

said, "I know you two want to be alone. I'm going to fix you breakfast in the morning. I want you two to come over and eat with me. Have a good night."

At last they were alone together. No one to disturb them. No one to fear. It was like being in paradise. It was like sailing together on a slow boat to China. It was a moment they had waited for all these years. And their stored-up emotions for each other could finally have its way. It was a night they would never forget.

Their hostess was superb. The breakfast she had prepared for them was exceptional. The minister carried them back to the railroad station, and they put Violet on the train to Chicago. Since Jason's train did not leave for some time later, the preacher and Jay got a copy made of the license, and Jay took the license and caught the train.

Mose met him at Red Bluff with the horse. Jason went by Aunt Millipus' house, told her what had happened, and asked her to keep his license in her trunk. Aunt Millipus was beaming with joy. As a matter of fact, she shouted a little bit.

"Thank God," she cried. "You outfoxed the fox—Ole Sam Moore. If he has a heart attack, he had it coming. God bless y'all and I'm going to give you two a present. Jay, you got a good wife and I'll say this. She's a lucky girl to get a husband like you. Matter of fact, she got the best boy and the best looking young man in Texas."

Jay went home and told his mother what had happened. He thought at last that Violet Moore was now Mrs. Violet Winfield.

Chapter 8

The House Jay Built

From the first day of his marriage Jay looked forward to building a house for Violet and himself. His business of cutting down and selling trees was profitable, but he had a longing to go into the sawmill business. That is, making lumber on his own place. It was a blessing that came to him one day when Chester Winfield was home visiting his grandmother. He came to see Jay and his little business. It was then that Chester, listening to Jay and hearing him wanting to start a lumberyard, took an interest in Jay's dream of having a lumberyard for himself.

He said, "Jay, I think I can help you. I know a man in deep East Texas who has been in the lumbering business and he has gotten old and sick and wants to sell out. I believe I could help you get that equipment and possibly ship it here on a train. You know I've always wanted to do something special for your family. I have an interest in a law firm and without me telling you you know my grandfather left my grandmother and me in good shape. We have lots of money. It was your father, Wade, who saved my life when I went and slipped in the tank to go swimming. I would have drowned had he not rescued me. And he did so much for my grandfather. I would just like to do something to say thanks to the memory of the best man that I ever knew.

He taught me so many things—how to ride a horse, how to swim, and how to paddle a boat. I would like to help you Jay. I am asking you—let me help you. And I know Grandma wouldn't mind."

Jay was all ears and said, "Mr. Chester, just give me a chance. If you'll do this for me—it may take a while—I'll pay your money back."

And so it was that a few months later Jay was set up to make lumber on his property. He did not know until he started setting up his business that Buck Jones was a lumberjack. Buck asked him for a job. He was still living alone at the same place and had experience from a lumberyard in Arkansas. Jay was so happy to take him on. And he found out quickly that Buck knew how to operate gasoline motors, saws, and planers. Buck was a hard working man and really another blessing to Jay. Everytime Jay made a board, he was thinking about a dream house that he would build for himself and Violet. He now had a small crew working for him. Even Mose worked part-time for him. He got contracts to sell lumber and old man Koohne bought lumber from him. With his farm, his cattle, and his trappings, it was quite evident that Jason Winfield was on his way to being a successful man. He worked hard and far into the night. He went up early in the morning before daylight to take care of his cows. He had increased his herd of cows to almost a 100. Now people were saying that he wasn't interested in women anymore, and they could not see a man so young just thinking about making a dollar. He seemed satisfied to go to work for six days a week. He and his mother and family would go to church on Sundays. When they came home he went back to one of his jobs. People even said that maybe he just didn't like women, which was the opposite of what they had said about him months earlier. But they could not know that he was married and that in another year Violet would be home. Then they would know why he maintained his moral principles in relationship to women with whom he could easily have had an affair.

It was one day while he and Mose were working that Mose suddenly said to him, "Jay, I want to take off early this evening. I have something to do."

Jay said, "No problem Mose. You want to tell me what it is? You know you don't have to."

"No," he said, "I don't mind telling you. I am going to go

home early and clean up. Then I'm going down to Uncle Frank Cotton's house and ask him and his wife permission to come see his daughter."

Surprisingly, Jay said, "Well, you are already going down there to see her without asking them permission."

Mose said, "Look, when they give me permission then that means she won't go out with nobody but me."

Jay said, "You thinking about getting married?"

"Well," Mose replied, "I guess I am."

Jay laughed, "Mose are you serious? What brought all of this about—or do I need to guess?"

"Well," Mose said, "You think you are smart anyhow. Just go ahead and guess." Jay said, "First of all, I think you are in love with Ellie. That's number one. And number two, I think you are jealous."

Mose said, "Go on, let me hear what you have to say."

Jay said, "There is a boy that's been coming across the river on a horse visiting Ellie too."

There was a custom that when the river was low there were some boys who would ride their horses across the river and visit girls on this side of the river. It was no secret that one of these boys was definitely interested in Ellie. He seemed to be a very nice young man. He had good manners, was clean, and knew that he had the respect of Uncle Frank and Josie.

Ellie and Nellie were twins. But Mose, even though they looked a lot alike, was dead serious about Ellie. He said to Jay, "I guess you got it pretty well right. A man is supposed to be jealous about someone he's interested in. Would you be jealous if you found out another guy was interested in Violet?"

"I'd have a right to be Mose, she's my wife," Jay said.

"You mean, you have never been jealous of her before y'all married?" Mose asked.

"Mose," Jay said, "Go on and take off right now. I am glad that somebody has conquered your heart. I can see you are in love with Ellie, and I think Uncle Frank and Aunt Josie are going to say yes."

During that time, if parents gave the boy permission to come and see their daughter, that meant whatever happened he was held responsible and no other boy could come and see her or take her anywhere. But Jay thought to himself, I am glad that he's gotten serious about Ellie. Jay didn't realize that later on this relationship would play into his hands.

90

Lucinda, Jay's mother, was very helpful to Jay. Often she fixed meals for the whole crew. She had a yard full of a variety of chickens. Her favorite was the Rhode Island Reds because they grew large, and there were times when she would fry a small dishpan full of chicken and take other foods down for a meal to the workers. They loved her cooking.

It was a little surprising, which probably shouldn't have been, because the old cliché said the way to a man's heart is through his stomach. The surprise was that Buck Jones became interested in Jay's mother Lucinda. He talked to Jay about it. Buck seemed to have made a complete about-face in his lifestyle. He had given up gambling, had gotten rid of his fighting roosters, was really dedicated to the lumber mill, and knew what he was doing. He had won the respect of Jay and the folks he worked with.

Jay said to Buck, "Look Buck, I'll say this, I love my mother very much and guess I never quite got over my father's death, but I know he's not coming back. Are you about forty years old?"

Buck replied, "Yeah you're right on it."

"Well," Jay continued, "Mom is still in her late thirties and I know she's young enough to have companionship, so I don't want to be selfish. Nobody will ever take papa's place with me, but I would not want her to go on living without having some kind of life for herself. So I think you need to talk that over with her. Whatever her decision is, I'll live with it."

The big surprise in the community that spring was Jay building a new house on his new property from the front side between his momma's house and the crossroad. There was much speculation. Some said he was building a new house for his momma. Others said he was going to build a house and live by himself because the rumor was that Cindy and Buck Jones were going to get married. Violet wrote him two and three letters a week, and he sent money orders to her private post office mailbox. He wrote and told her that he was building them a house, and if she had any ideas about what she wanted to write him and let him know. That is where he got many of his ideas. He also got some of his ideas from Aunt Millipus. She had lived in a colonial mansion in Jackson Quarters before they built her a little house in the back. The Griffins had a beautiful home that Aunt Millipus had worked in, and she and Violet, who lived in a nice home in Chicago with her auntie, had a lot to do with the house decor. Violet wanted a large parlor, a dining room, three bedrooms, a kitchen, a small hallway, and a storage and washroom. She also wanted a large front porch that went half way across the house and back porch. Aunt Millipus suggested the height of the walls, the size of the windows, and the color of the house, which naturally was white. Jay even put lightning rods on the house to keep lightning bolts from striking it. He dug a well in the back yard and bought a small windmill complete with a pump. When the wind would blow, it would turn the windmill and the windmill would pump the water out of the well. He piped water to his house. He also built a smokehouse and a buggy shed attached to it. It was the talk of the community, but because he was in the lumber business and because Buck Jones was a good carpenter, he got by much cheaper than he would have otherwise. He even bought a bedroom suite and a cook stove and with Buck's help he made a kitchen table. He had a large fireplace in Violet's parlor.

He moved into his house and lived alone. Folks shook their heads and asked why he wanted to live in this big house by himself with only a bedroom suite, a fireplace, and a homemade table. But only his mother, Aunt Millie, and Mose knew the whole story. They were loyal to him, and it was a secret he kept from the rest of the people. Even Uncle Sam Cotton drove down there one day on his old gray horse, rode up into the woods, and looked at his house, and his lumber mill. When he came back, he met Uncle Frank on the road. He stopped and told him that he had to give it to Jay for being a hard-working man. But it didn't hardly make any sense for him to be living in that big house by himself. He didn't understand it. He said he hoped he wasn't going crazy. He said he really had a nice place.

Mose and Ellie became engaged. This was also news. Mose Randolph and Ellie Cotton were getting married. Nellie had chosen to go to high school in a town about twenty miles away because now the three-teacher school went to the nineth grade. To finish high school they had to go to another black high school out of town. The wedding would not be until June. Nellie would be home at that time, and she would be the maid of honor. Of course, Jay would naturally be the best man, which at that time they called the waiter.

Things had begun to change and Jason, Aunt Millipus, Lucinda, and Mrs. Randolph had talked Buck Jones into going to church sometimes. It was a new experience for him because he had never been a member of the church. But he would go either to the Methodist or to the Baptist church. People like Uncle Frank, who was a steward in the Methodist church, or Deacon Randolph in the Baptist church, always made him feel welcome.

During the first part of May the community started getting ready to celebrate the nineteenth of June. Every man gave one dollar, and with this money they bought a large calf to barbecue and soda water. The women cooked the rest of the food for the free dinner. One of the young men or young women in the community alternated each year and recited the Emancipation Proclamation.

They had a big celebration. Ball games, picnics, speeches, and then a program at night where the young ladies from the community and those home from college would sing. They would sing such songs as "Oh, Freedom, Oh Freedom . . ." and "Before I'd be a slave, I'd be Buried in my grave and go home to my Lord and be saved."

Each man in the community gave a dollar to help buy a yearling calf to barbecue and some sodas to drink for the picnic.

In 1897 the nineteenth of June fell on a Saturday, and big things were planned for the entire weekend. On Friday night the men would barbecue a calf bought by money donated to the nineteenth of June club members. Ole man Richard Koohne also gave either two goats or a hog for the celebration. It was good business for him. He usually showed up for dinner.

A pit was dug on the school ground and a heavy metal screen was placed over the hole to cook the meat on. Underneath the screen was oak or pecan tree wood to cook and smoke the meat.

It was an all-night job, but it was even more exciting to the people who had already started celebrating Friday evening. The Saturday festivities began promptly at 10 o'clock in the morning. The men had built a huge arbor with a platform for the speaker, which would be used for the Saturday night dance.

The feature attraction of the morning was the special presentation and recognition of a family or a person in the community whom they recognized as having made or was making outstanding achievements that complimented Crossroads.

This particular year the honoree was the Mike Washington family who lived at the south end of Dogwood Lane, which ended or began as the case might be at Crossroad and changed to Red Bluff Lane.

The Washington's owned three hundred acres of land, with most of it being river bottom and the rest was about twenty acres setting on a hill overlooking the river some distance away. Mike Washington was a successful farmer with horses, mules, and a number of cattle. His house was a two-story structure with a porch and balcony that sat with dignity on their precipice—it offered a grand view of the beautiful farm and the lazy winding river.

Amanda Home Washington, his wife, who was called Miss Mandy by most people, was much younger than her husband Uncle Mike. She was a good housewife. She had taught school in the one-room building for a number of years before the county consolidated it with the Crossroad School. She and her husband had seven boys and one daughter and all were there for the occasion.

Mrs. Randolph, through her maneuvering, was given the honor of presenting the Washington family. And even though they were good friends, it was common knowledge that they were generally accepted as the two best-dressed women in the community. Mrs. Randolph planned it all well. She walked gracefully to the stage and allowed one of the young men to assist her as she mounted the steps to the platform.

She was dressed in a two-piece suit. It was a blue and white polka dotted Swiss outfit with the open coat extending down to her finger-length. She had a triple string of blue beads that fell below a full bust. Her hair was combed backward and upward into what they called a fan. Her high-heeled slippers clicked on the floor as she walked to a position in the middle of the floor.

Bowing slightly, she began. "Good morning, ladies and gentlemen. I feel so highly honored to present the family that the committee has chosen to honor this year as the outstanding citizens of our community in 1897. They have achieved so much and have made so many great contributions, not only in the local area, but also to East Texas, and I daresay to the whole great state of Texas.

"Mrs. Washington has informed me that her husband Mr. Mike Washington does the talking at home, and he lets her do the public speaking. Having been in the school room for a number of years and having raised eight children, I feel comfortable in saying she is well able. So I am going to present to you Mrs. Amanda Washington who will introduce to some of you and present to others her lovely family. Mrs. Washington . . . . Give her a hand."

Mrs. Washington, with the assistance of the young man, mounted the stairs where Mrs. Randolph was awaiting her. They embraced and kissed and Mrs. Randolph took her seat on the stage. Mrs. Washington turned her body ever so slightly to thank her friend and then turned slowly but deliberately to the audience. She was confidently dressed in a soft pink tunic suit with a black and white sash that was tied at her side by some kind of large fancy pin. The ends of the sash hung down to the end of her tunic.

She was wearing a string of large, expensive pearls around her neck and both her hat and shoes were black and white. Because of her youthful-looking, well-kept body, if for no other reason, she had the edge on Mrs. Randolph. After thanking the committee and the community for honoring her family, she promptly began her introduction. "First of all let me present the gentleman who, except for Jesus Christ, is the best thing that ever happened in my life, my husband Mr. Mike Washington."

The crowd applauded as he mounted the steps. She continued, "And now I present our oldest son, Mike Jr., better known to his old friends as Buddy Mike. He is a graduate of Prairie View Industrial College and has come back home. He purchased some land, built a house, has a cattle ranch, and is married to a beautiful young lady of whom I am very proud. Come children." The audience applauded again.

"Our second son is Booker T. . . . known to his friends as B.T. He too is a graduate of Prairie View and is an English teacher at the high school in Tyler, Texas. His lovely wife and two children are with him. Come Booker.

"Our third son is a preacher. He is a graduate of Bishop College at Marshall, Texas, and is pastoring a large church in Conroe, Texas. He is Rev. A. L. or Abe Lincoln Washington. I present to you him, his wife and son.

"Our fourth son is George and is attending Tuskeegee Institute in Alabama where he received a four-year scholarship. Come A.L."

"Our fifth son . . . I hope you are not getting tired . . . he is J.J. or Jack Johnson. He received a scholarship from and is attending Wiley College at Marshall. So you see we have both Baptists and Methodists in the family.

"Our sixth son, J. B. or John Brown, is attending Prairie

View. He is working his way through school on the farm there. And our baby boy is the twin of our one daughter, Martha. They didn't want to be far apart so they both are freshmen in Waco, Texas. He is attending Central Texas Baptist College—west side of the Brazos and she is attending Paul Quinn A.M.E. College on the east side of the Brazos in Waco. Both of these are in McLennan County.

"Incidentally, my youngest brother, Clem Horne, was swallowed up in death by the Brazos River just one year ago. It happened fifteen miles south of Waco on a farm on the river's west side. That's in northern Falls County near a predominantly colored settlement called Bulls' Quarters where I still have distant relatives. I still have a clipping from the Waco newspaper, the *Waco Morning News,* which my relatives mailed to me about the drowning. The newspaper reported that the drowning happened on Thursday, June 11, 1896. In the envelope are the names of some of the family members of their church, some of whom might have attended the funeral in another community. I vaguely remember some of the family names, such as the Buhls, Masters, Londons, Graves, Wells, Buyer, and a lady named Mandy Milsap, none of whom I was ever fortunate to meet."

She choked in her voice and the people recognized this was still a painful memory. She composed herself and said, "Oh, I'm sorry, this is to be a happy occasion. Oh, I almost forgot, our baby son's name . . . it is Prince Hall, P. A., Washington. He has already made up his mind that he wants to make his home in Waco. When he finishes college he wants to teach in the prestigious Negro high school in South Waco, just a short distance south of the famous suspension bridge. It is the only such kind in this great state of Texas. The school is located on the west side of the river."

She continued, "But I really think that he has his eyes and his heart set on one of the many beautiful young ladies in the affluent colored community on Baptist Hill in North Waco where his school is located. On the other hand, Martha Phillis, our only daughter wants to be a music teacher. She has been playing the piano since she was five years old. I taught her piano in my home and there is a word that fits her. I believe it is adept which means she is extra ordinarily skillful and she can teach someone something and in time that person can do it better than her. That is what has happened with Phillis. She can play a ring around me. She wants to be near her twin brother, so she wants to stay in Waco and give piano lessons to young people in East Waco, which now is growing fast and is on its way to being an enormous social Negro community in Central Texas. This is our family."

There was applause from the audience.

"Mike Junior's son, Theodore, will give a recitation that will end our presentation. Come darling," she said. "He is ten years old."

Theodore stepped forward in a white shirt with a drawstring at the bottom. He had on a pair of light gray wool pants that ended just below his knees. There were buckles on the band of his pants that served to tighten around his legs and formed a little blouse. His shoes and socks were the best of that day. He stepped forward, bowed, and said, "I shall name the six New England States, their capitals and the river or bodies in or at the capitals. They are, Maine Agusta on the Kenebac River, New Hampshire Concord on the Merrimac, Vermont Mt. Peiler on the Winooski and Massachusetts, Boston on the Boston Bay, Rhode Island Providence on the Providence Bay, and Connecticut Hartford on the Connecticut River. And as for our state of Texas, which joined the Union in 1836 and is the largest state in the Union, the city of Austin is the capital on the Colorado River. Thank you."

Mrs. Randolph came forward and said, "Let's give the family a big hand. Thank you Mistress Washington for your information. My husband has some relatives in Falls County in or near Marlin, which is the county seat. I am sure that you know that the famous Falls on the Brazos River was how the county got its name." This was her way of letting people know that she, too, had some geographical knowledge of the state of Texas.

They all gave the Washington's a standing ovation. She signaled to a young man in the audience to bring a large cardboard box wrapped in brown paper to the stage. This was the gift from the community to the Washington family. The community had raised the money by having a community supper and had ordered the gift out of a mail-order catalogue. Mrs. Amanda opened the box, tore the tissue paper from around the contents, and to her and her family's delight it was a large grandfather clock that struck in time each hour of the day. She kissed Mrs. Randolph and graciously thanked the community.

It was a big affair and as usual hardly any black people worked on that day. People bought their children new clothes, held their ball games, and as usual had speakers. Some of the young men got together and talked the committee into letting them have a dance on the school ground. They persuaded Buck Jones and three of his friends to furnish the music for the dance. Buck Jones was a little hesitant because since he started going to church he had a different perspective about living, as church people should. But he finally consented to get his old buddies together. One played a guitar; another played a washboard, and another the drums.

That night they had a peaceful but very festive dance. No fights and nobody getting drunk and raising sand. It was a compliment to the community. Some of the people all but twisted Buck Jones' arm trying to get him to sing one of the old blues songs. He finally decided to do a small part of a number that they had heard him sing before. After his piano introduction he started playing, and to the accompaniment of the other three he began to sing, "I hate to see that evening sun go down, because the gal I love she's done left this town." People always wondered if he got those words from Jesse Handy who wrote the St. Louis blues or was it the other way around. Had Handy heard Buck sing the song and made his award-winning song? He sang a little of the song and then cut it off because people thought he was really singing about Clara Bell.

Sunday night was the wedding night for Mose and Ellie. Mrs. Randolph talked with Aunt Josie, and they decided to have the wedding at the Baptist church because it was larger than the Methodist church. It had nice pews, and Mrs. Randolph was anxious to decorate this church herself. She invited friends from the city. She invited Professor Love and Geraldine to the wedding. Aunt Josie had them write to Leola in California to come to the wedding. It was some kind of affair that they had planned. Deacon Randolph was going to kill a hog for the dinner. They had Ellie and Nellie's dresses made. Jay and Mose had suits alike. The Baptist and Methodist preachers were going to perform the ceremony. It was the social function of the year because the Randolph's were what you call big Negroes in the community. The Cottons were not that far behind. People came out of the bottom from the other side of Koohne's Town, out of the bottoms in wagons, from across the river on horses. It was some kind of affair and Saturday night, before the wedding, Violet came home on the train.

The women spent most of the evening after church decorating for the wedding, which was scheduled for around 7 o'clock in the evening. The house was packed, and at the given time Mose and Ellie came in and stood at the altar. Then the flower girls entered dropping red and white rose petals as they came down the aisles. Mrs. Love played the new piano and down the aisle came Jason walking with Ellie. Mr. and Mrs. Randolph were on the front seat with the family. Uncle Frank and Aunt Josie were on the front seat on the other side. As Mrs. Love started playing "Here Comes the Bride" everybody rose and stood until the bride and groom reached the altar, and then the preacher asked, "Who giveth this woman?" Uncle Frank stood up and said, "I do." Then the wedding took place.

Ellie was in a white dress with a long train. She looked very beautiful. At the end of the ceremony the preacher prayed and then told the bridegroom to kiss the bride. Mose took her in his arms and kissed her tenderly and the minister said, "Ladies and gentlemen, I present to you, Mr. and Mrs. Mose Randolph Jr."

The people were applauding. At that time Mrs. Love started playing the music again and suddenly, before Mose and Ellie could move, the preacher said, "I have an important announcement to make. In this audience is another young bride. I am going to ask her to stand and come forward, and since she was unable to have a church wedding previously, she and her husband are going to repeat their vows tonight. That person is none other than the former Miss Violet Cotton who is really now and has been for the past year, Mrs. Violet Winfield, whose husband is Jason Winfield. Mrs. Winfield will you please come forward?"

The shock of the audience was terrific. There were ohs and ahs and whats. The crowd was surprised when Violet came forward, dressed in a white suit and a blouse with ruffles down the front. She looked very pretty. People did not know what to say. The preacher said, "Mr. Winfield, may I have the license?"

Aunt Millipus, who was sitting on the second row stood up, handed the license to Jay. Jay handed it to the preacher. The preacher read the license and the date it was signed. Then they repeated their vows. Even Mrs. Randolph did not know about this wedding. How could they put this by her? Even Uncle Sam was at the wedding. He stood there looking as if he was lost.

Then the two couples walked out of the church. As they marched out a voice in an obscure corner of the church was heard saying, "Amen, and ain't nobody mad but the devil." And everybody knew that that was Lazarus.

At the reception, after all the congratulations and so forth, Jason and Mose went to change clothes. When they returned they ran into Leola.

Leola said to Jason, "Jason I want to congratulate you. You and Violet looked so beautiful tonight and I am very happy for you. I have to be honest and tell you that I don't regret our past relationship, but that is in the past. I have met somebody who I hope will fill the void in my life. In the meantime I hope the best for you and your bride. God knows that I mean it. I am saying goodbye."

Jason said, "Thank you for all of the things you have done. You helped me in my studies and gave me something to hold on to. You also helped me in my spiritual and emotional life, and I shall never forget you. And one more thing, whoever that fellow is that it seems you are going to say your vows to, I would say that he is the luckiest man on the California gold coast."

Leola looked up at him with watery eyes, thinking of what might have been, touched his hand, and said softly, "Thank you Jason." She then moved away into the crowd.

In less than ten minutes, Mrs. Love came over to where he was and said, "Jason, I have never said this to you, but I want to congratulate you on your success in life at such an early age. And I want to congratulate you on your bride. Leola is a charming and intelligent young woman and she has airs and grace. I can see how she would be charmed by your physique, your demeanor, and those beautiful eyes. Violet has the freshness of youth and she is also intelligent, and when you add all of this to her beauty, I would have to say that you certainly made the right choice because I think that she will put Leola in the shade. So have a happy life, Jay."

Jason and Violet, as he had already arranged, caught the train the same night after the wedding and went to San Antonio on their honeymoon. Mose and Ellie went to spend a couple days with a distant cousin of Mose's, not too far away.

Professor Love took Aunt Millipus back to the city with him where she made and drew up her will. She stayed the rest of the week with the Loves, and he brought her back home on the train. She gave him a copy of the will; they put one in the safe deposit box at the bank and the other one in her trunk. Jason and Violet came home and went shopping to buy furniture to set up housekeeping. Aunt Clara came and helped with the furniture in the house. They were very happy. The wedding seemed to have even drawn Mose and his wife and Violet and Jay closer. After all Mose and Violet were cousins.

The annual revival was in August—known then as the protracted meeting. Most folks said "tracted meeting." The word revival became more popular later on. They would have prayer meeting one whole week. The next week the visiting preacher would come for five or six nights to preach. It always began on Monday. That's when all of the young people or whoever didn't belong to church would go to the mourner's bench seeking to be saved. Aunt Millipus, Deacon Randolph's wife, Mrs. Cotton, and Lucinda talked Buck Jones into going to the mourner's bench. They prayed for him and urged him to believe the Bible, be converted, and join the church. He sat there for five nights on the bench. Others were getting up and he just sat there. On that Friday night the preacher preached about Paul and Silas in jail and they were singing and praying. At the end of the sermon one of the other preachers sang a song about Jesus. There was something about the song that must have touched the heartstring of Buck. He stood up and for half a minute just stood there. He then stepped forward and gave the preacher his hand. And you might have thought that someone had dropped a bombshell in the church.

Everyone was shouting and Aunt Millipus jumped up off of her seat, ran down the aisle, threw her cane away, and someone said, "Grab her, she's going to fall without that walking stick."

She said, "Let me alone."

It was some kind of night. That Sunday, they baptized Buck and the other candidates in the river.

Chapter 9

Aunt Millipus Dies

About three miles down the road that crossed Sandy Lane was a one-room school called Willow Grove. Many of the people who lived in this community had moved up to Sandy Lane while others had moved to the river bottom to farm the land as sharecroppers. They had their own mules and horses so they farmed the land thirds and fourths, which meant that if you had your own tools and animals you received two thirds of the corn at harvest time and three fourths of the cotton. That's where the term third and fourth came from.

Since most of the people had left Willow Grove, the school trustees decided to tear down the school and consolidate it with Sandy Lane. This is the school where Mrs. Amanda Washington taught for nine years. They built another room on to the Sandy Lane School, hired Violet as one of the teachers, and added the eighth and ninth grades. Sandy Lane now became a junior high school. This was a complement to the community even though most of the books that they had came from the white high school in Koohne Town.

Aunt Millipus, who had had a very successful year with her garden, often cooked food and sold it to the carpenters who were working at the school. They all loved her cooking. She made cakes, pies, and molasses bread. She even made biscuits and put homemade sausage between them. They loved it. She became an entrepreneur in her own right. Along with selling things out of her garden and kitchen, she still had time to deliver babies for people in the community all the way up to Red Bluff. From a catalog she ordered such things as liniment, salves, pills, and the like. She resold them to the people in the neighborhood. She always carried some kind of medicine when she went to deliver babies or to doctor on someone who might have been sick.

It was during this time that old man Richard Koohne gave the church a huge steel bell that his father had owned when he ran his plantation. He had used it to ring for the slaves to go into the fields in the morning, at lunchtime, and late in the evening when it was time to quit. Since the new church did not have a steeple, it became necessary for them to build a bell tower and so carpenters were employed to build a tower on the church and a steeple on the top of the tower. When the tower was completed and they were ready to hang the bell, they invited Mr. Koohne to witness the event. It was on a Saturday, and they solicited the help of the younger men to use ropes and chains to lift this heavy bell from the ground to the tower. It was a memorable occasion and because of the number of men that were there, Aunt Millipus dug some sweet potatoes out of her garden and made potato pies to sell to the workers. Out of courtesy old man Koohne bought a slice of the pie. When he had eaten it, he liked it so well that he wanted to buy a whole pie. He asked Aunt Millipus to make him some pies the next week and told her if she couldn't bring them to him he would send someone after them. That's how her little business expanded. From that time on, every week she could sell more pies in town than she was able to make.

It was rather strange but occasionally somebody would hear a screech owl in the night, and it always brought a pain in Jay's heart. When he heard a screech owl or, as many people called it, a death owl, sure enough in weeks or in days the bell would ring and somebody had passed on. There were nights when Jay would hear the owl and wonder who would be the next to go. He did not have to wonder very long, because one morning somebody came fastly riding a horse and told Jay to tell Violet that her mother had passed. Violet took it hard. Since Uncle Sam was getting feeble, he decided that he could no longer live by himself. Since all of the children had left home and Bonnie, Violet's brother, was staying in the city, Violet was left with the responsibility of taking her father in her home. Many people said, "Who would have thought that old man Sam who hated Jay would finally wind up living with him."

Aunt Millipus told him to his face, "What goes over the horse's back comes around under his belly. Now I guess you see how you treated Jay. That's why it pays to treat people right. For when you cast your bread on the water one of these days it will come back to you."

No matter how busy he was Jason always went by to see Aunt Millipus. She always wanted him to plow her garden, plow up her potatoes, and build her potato kill. The potato kill was made out of hay, corn stalks, and covered with dirt like a teepee. This kill protected the potatoes from all types of weather.

It was during this time of the year that the community had the big surprise. Lucinda and Buck Jones got married. This turned out to be a blessing to the whole family.

It was Thanksgiving Day that the Randolphs invited Aunt Millipus to dinner. Mose went to get her because he insisted that she didn't need to walk over there. Beaming with joy as he helped Aunt Millipus in the buggy he said, "Aunt Millipus I have something to tell you."

"I am going to be a father," he said.

Aunt Millipus laughed and said, "Boy I been knowing that. That gal come over here one morning and puked like a dog. And I knew then that she was going to have a baby. But I am glad for you."

Even though he was disappointed that he hadn't surprised Aunt Millipus, that did not dampen his happiness and he said, "I want a boy. And if it's a boy I ain't going to name him Mose."

"Why," she said.

"Well," he said. "I think two Moses in a family is enough. Anyway we'll wait to see what it is. But you'll have the job of delivering the baby when the time comes."

It seemed ironic that both Violet and Lucinda became pregnant about a month later. So it seemed that Aunt Millipus had her work cut out for her. Since school did not start until the first of October, Violet stayed out of school the first month after the baby was born, and then Lucinda kept the baby and nursed both on her breast. Both Mose and Jay and their wives had boys. Lucinda and Buck had a girl.

When Christmas came again Victoria came home from college. This was her senior year. She would be graduating the last of May. She had already been promised a job teaching at the high school in Koohne Town to the delight of old man Koohne and his wife. They looked on Victoria as their own daughter because of her and Trey's relationship. Anyway, she went to see Aunt Millie again, and again she stayed a long time. People were used to her going to see Aunt Millipus but were curious as to why she stayed so long. But Aunt Millipus said not a word, not even to Jay about these strange visits to her from Victoria.

As time went by, Mose and Ellie had a second child. Jay's business was going well and Aunt Millipus was still cooking, selling food, and delivering babies. The word got out that Aunt Millipus had finally completed her will. Victoria was teaching English in the high school in Koohne Town, and her engagement to Richard the III or Trey had been announced and the wedding indeed would be in June.

By this time Aunt Millipus' health had begun to fade. Jay visited her everyday to see how she was doing. Sometimes it might have been nine o'clock at night, but he always went to see her before he went to bed. Then early one morning he went to see her and found her lying across the bed. She was dead. This saddened the entire community.

Her funeral was one of the largest ever held in the community. As soon as the funeral procession of wagons, surreys, buggies, and even horseback riders left Aunt Millipus' house on its way to the church, Uncle Lum Webb, a former slave of the Webb family—and who was above eighty years old—went into the little room where the rope from the bell tower descended, and as he had done in the past years, began to ring the bell. He had an art of his own for ringing the bell. On Sunday mornings he would ring it with a certain slow rhythmic sound, and the people recognized that he was calling members to come to worship. When rung on weekdays it had a more rapid continuous sound signaling a warning of a storm or an overflow and people knew to take shelter or move to higher ground. He would always ring it the same way on the nineteenth of June morning in celebration of the Emancipation Proclamation. On Christmas morning and at 12 o'clock midnight on New Year's Eve, he rang the old year out and the new year in. Whenever there was a death in the community he would toll the bell. One ring and then a pause and then two successive ones. He repeated this over and over and many people would speak almost under their breath alone with the sad toll . . . dead and gone, dead and gone, dead and gone.

Now he continued the tone until the casket was taken off the wagon and the deacons who were pallbearers took her body into the church. Only then did Uncle Lum stop the bell ringing and the echoes of the sound of the steel bell faded in the ears of the community for miles around.

Parson Prince, who had led the procession down the aisle, now stood behind the pulpit in his frock-tail coat with the two buttons in the back and gave out the hymn in a poetic form: "If I must die, oh let me die in peace with all mankind," to which the congregation joined in solemn singing.

There were only a few dry eyes in the congregation at the end of the hymn. Jason, Violet, and the Webb family sat on the front bench representing Aunt Millipus' family. Only Jason, Professor Love, and Victoria knew that as far as they knew, Victoria was her only living relative.

Both whites and blacks came. The crowd overflowed the church and people were all outdoors. From on the other side of town all the way up to Red Bluff down in the river bottom they came. Many people made remarks and paid tribute to what they felt like was one of the great humanitarians that had lived in the community. Her name was even put in the newspaper.

After they deposited the body in the grave and covered it up, the people slowly dispersed. Walter and Marie Webb stood a few yards from the grave talking with Lucinda and Buck. Victoria went to her buggy, got a vase with some roses in it, and placed it on top of the grave. She stood there alone for a few minutes. Her mother and father did not bother her because they knew how much she loved Aunt Millipus and how Aunt Millipus had loved her.

While she stood there, of all people, Lazarus came by and spoke to the Webbs and Buck Jones and Lucinda. They were speechless. He was surprisingly dressed in a pair of hustler-stripped pants, a collarless white shirt, and a dark coat. He went to the grave of Aunt Millipus while Violet was still standing there alone. He stooped down and made a small indention at the head of the grave and placed a twig that he had picked from an evergreen tree.

Still stooping, he looked up at Victoria and said, "She was a good woman . . . an honest woman, and like this cedar twig, she will live forever." Still stooping down, he put a little more

106

dirt around the twig and then he said in a voice that was almost a whisper, "I am glad she found you." With that he stood up, turned his back, and walked away. Then he said loud enough for everyone to hear, "She's at rest and ain't nobody mad but the devil." He went around the back of the church toward the outer house and was out of sight.

Professor Love told Jay that he was going to stay until Thursday since this was Sunday when they buried her. At Aunt Millipus' request, he would read the will. By that time he would have notified all person's who were beneficiaries.

Chapter 10

The Reading of Aunt Millipus' Will

By Thursday all parties had been notified that the will would be read in a local lawyer's office. This lawyer had given Professor Love some advice as to probating the will. They were all there. Jay and Violet, Mose and Ellie and the two children, Lucinda and Buck Jones, Reverend Prince, Elder Scruggs, and Victoria Webb. Professor Love made a short speech indicating what a wonderful person Aunt Millipus was, and that this was her last will and testament, which had been witnessed and notarized by a lawyer's secretary in the city. He had one copy, Aunt Millipus had a copy, and with his suggestion, Aunt Millipus had rented a safety deposit box at the bank where her money was and only she and Professor Love had keys to the box. Then he read the will:

To the churches I leave $50.00, each which should to be used to buy a new pulpit and chairs.
To Buck and Lucinda Jones I will my milk cow.
To Mose and Ellie Randolph I will my horse.
To Victoria Webb I will all of my jewelry, my trunk and a key to the trunk.
To Jason and Violet Winfield I will my acre and a half of land, my house and everything in it, except the items for

Victoria, and two hundred acres of land in Cherokee County, Texas.

The keys to the trunk would be given to Jay after Professor Love had unlocked it. The jewelry and a key, which had been given to Victoria, were also in the trunk.

It was then that two white men appeared on the scene. One was a lawyer who was representing the other. The lawyer said that he had proof that the will for the two hundred acres of land was not valid. He had gone to the judge and had requested a lawsuit, specifically because of the two hundred acres being put in the will. He felt the will was not valid. If need be he would pay the court costs. He also stated that he was representing the original family who implemented the deed that was in question.

The judge granted the request and set the trial date for thirty days later. At the request of the lawyers the trial would be held without a jury, and the judge would decide the ruling. It came as a shock or perhaps a double shock because none of these people knew that Aunt Millipus had two hundred acres of land in Texas. It sounded preposterous to say the least. And who was this strange man who had come into the community indicating that Aunt Millipus had lied? Was he a crook and possibly a criminal?

These were shocking things. Everybody looked forward to being at the trial when it was held. As mysteriously as these two men came, they disappeared with the assurance that they would be back in thirty days.

When the day of the trial came the courthouse was packed. Whites were seated on one side and blacks on the other. The Webbs were present to name a few. Old man Richard Koohne and his wife were there and seated on the side reserved for whites only. She was all dressed up with all of her jewelry on. Buck and Lucinda were there. Mose and his wife and children were there for the trial. Even old man Randolph and his wife were there. Jay and Violet and their baby and many other people were there. At the given moment Judge Griffin sounded the gavel and called the court to order.

He said, "The George Jackson family versus the Authenticity of the will of one Millie Stone."

The judge asked the lawyer for the plaintiff—family of George Jackson—to come forward and read his opening statement. The lawyer came forward and began by saying that he had proof that Millie Stone was born in Louisiana and was the slave of one George Jackson, who was supposed to have committed suicide with a self-inflicted gunshot. He was also to have made out a will to Millie Stone and her two children before his death. The will included two hundred acres of land in Texas, which Millie Stone was to be a guardian over until the children were grown. They would then become inheritants of the provisions of the will. Millie Stone was the first person to find George Jackson dead. There was a question as to whether he really killed himself or whether she killed him in order to immediately claim this property. The will provided that the land could not be deeded to anyone outside of the family, nor could the three original persons on the will sell the land. He continued, "Miss Stone, your honor, under these provisions, could not will the land to any person because the deed also provided that if all parties passed away and there were no offsprings of the family that the land would go back to the original benefactors. And so in light of these facts, and I have a copy of the said deed which you can read, Miss Stone could not deed the property to anyone else. The property under the provisions would have to go back to the Jackson Estate. This, your honor, is my presentation."

Judge Griffin then told lawyer Winfield, who was the lawyer for the defense, to come forward and make his opening statement. Chester Winfield, dressed in a tweed suit, came forward.

He began by saying, "Your honor, I stand here today in defense of the integrity of a woman whom not only I knew as well as most of the people in this courtroom. She was a fine, honest, hard working, longtime citizen of our community. That woman's name was Millie Stone, who was sentimentally referred to as Aunt Millipus. She lived in this community for possibly the last twenty years and worked and attended to her own business. Aunt Millipus, if you please, made many friends and helped a lot of people in this area. Jason Winfield was one of those people she helped when he was just a small boy, because she felt she saw some special things in him. When she retired as housekeeper and nurse maid for the Walter and Marie Webb family and moved into her own home, Jason, who was a little boy at that time, helped her in her garden and in her yard, ran errands for her, cut wood, and carried it into her house for heat. So it was a continued relationship between him and Aunt Millipus. He always went to see about Aunt Millipus. He ran errands for her and took her to the grocery store and did whatever she needed him to do. Jason was always there. When he was seventeen years old, he assumed the responsibility of taking care of his widowed mother and his younger brothers and sisters. But he was never too busy to go by and see about an old lady who had befriended him and still gave him teacakes and whatever she had because of her fondness for Mr. Winfield. Since Miss Stone had no children before she passed on, she made out her will. It included her acre and a half of land and a house to Jason Winfield, and she also, as the lawyer for the plaintiff indicated, had two hundred acres of land, which had been deeded to her and her two children by her former white slave owner in Louisiana, a Mr. George Jackson. Since her children, as far as she knew, had both passed away, and since she had no offspring, (neither she nor the children), she made out a will to Jason Winfield for all of her property—that is land property. The will stipulated that the land could not be sold, deeded, nor willed to anyone outside of the offspring of those three persons whom the lawyer has pointed out. If all parties under these conditions passed away, the two hundred acres of land would go back to the Jackson Estate. Now, I highly respect the lawyer for the plaintiff, but I think there is a clause in this stipulation that might not have been examined to the fullest extent by him. There is one word in this particular clause that I don't think the gentleman gave enough attention to, because it stipulates that in case these parties die with no immediate inheritants the property would go back to the Jackson Estate. But I would like to call your attention to the fact that the two hundred acres was never a part of the Jackson Estate. Mr. Jackson purchased this land, paid cash, and had the deed made out in Texas to Aunt Millipus and her children, which is to say, your honor, that the property could not go back to the Jackson Estate because it never was a part of it. So this being the case I think we will all agree that you cannot go back to where you have never been. So then how could the property go back to the Jackson Estate when it never was a part of it? Perhaps this might have been a shrewd way that this Mr. Jackson was protecting the rights of the beneficiaries in the first place. I think the plaintiff might have overlooked this important word—back—which is the key to the right of the beneficiary to do whatever he or she pleases with the property. And so I stand here to say, based on these findings, that the land was Aunt Millipus', and she had a right to do what she did. I hope you will agree with me when I say that the will should stand as read. Thank you, your Honor."

At that point it was almost dinnertime. So the judge recessed until one o'clock when he would hear the witnesses. There were a lot of questions among the spectators. Naturally, the home people who had never heard Chester Winfield represent a client in a court setting were proud of him and felt like he had made a very good point. Promptly at one o'clock the judge called the court to order and asked the lawyer of the plaintiff to present his first witness.

The lawyer said, "I call Mr. Thomas Jefferson Black." Mr. Black came forward and the judge said, "You swear to tell the truth, the whole truth and nothing but the truth?"

He replied, "I do."

"State your name."

"Thomas Jefferson Black."

"You may be seated, Mr. Black and Lawyer Glass you may proceed," said the judge. Lawyer Glass began his inquiry.

"Mr. Black, did you know the lady in question, Miss Millie Stone?"

"No sir, I did not," he replied.

"Did you know the widow of this George Jackson?"

"I did."

"And how long have you known Mrs. Jackson?"

"We were schoolmates," he answered, "in Baton Rouge, Louisiana, from the time we were children."

"And did you know Mrs. Jackson's husband?"

"I had met him."

"And what then? You are representing him?"

"Yes, sir."

"And why?"

"Because she is a semi-invalid."

"And how did you come about representing Mrs. Jackson?"

"Well, after not being able to take care of herself on the plantation, she decided to move back to be closer to her doctors. And because of her situation she asked me to help her in finding somebody else to run the plantation and the business that was involved. She left that in the hands of what we call a straw boss. She moved out of the big house, she and her son, who unfortunately has a handicap. And when she moved all of her possessions out of the house, she found a trunk in the attic upstairs—that is her helper's found a trunk because she could not

112

go upstairs anymore. She found some keys to fit the trunk, and when they unlocked the trunk they found a copy of the deeds that Colonel Jackson had made to Aunt Millipus as they called her—on the deed is the name Millie Stone. When she had the deed examined by a lawyer, we found this stipulation about how the land could not be deeded, sold, or willed to anyone outside of the family. On the deed was the location of the land, the amount, and those to whom he deeded the property."

"So after all of these years, Mr. Black, how did you find out about Millie Stone being dead?"

"We checked at the courthouse in the county, and we checked in the tax office, and found out in recent years that the taxes were being paid by this Miss Stone by mail. We also found out where the mail came from. When we got the notice that she was dead and that she had no relatives, the property would revert back to the Jackson Estate."

"I see, and so your interest is because of a long-time relationship."

"That is correct, your honor."

"Thank you Mr. Black."

The Judge said to Mr. Winfield, "You may question the witness."

Chester Winfield stepped forward, papers in hand, and asked, "Mr. Black, did you say you knew Mr. Jackson?"

"Yes, he married in Baton Rouge and I was at the wedding."

"Did you ever visit the plantation—the Jackson Estate?"

"Well, no not really until Mrs. Jackson decided to move, and then I went out to help her get moved and help her get somebody in the big house."

"So it was that you did not really have that much relationship with Mr. Jackson."

"That is correct."

"So you did not know Miss Stone?"

"No, sir."

"Mr. Black, it seems a little unusual that you would take this kind of interest in someone who was just a causal friend. Would there be any other reason why you are doing this?"

Lawyer Glass said, "This question is irrelevant since this question had nothing to do with the will in question."

"Sustained," the judge said.

"Go on."

"Thank you judge. Then, are you related to this Mrs. Jackson?"

"No, I am not."

"So this then is just a good Samaritan deed on your part."

"Well, if that is the way you want to put it," he replied.

"Mr. Black, is it true, or are you aware of the fact that this property is in litigation?"

Lawyer Glass stands again. "Your honor, the question is irrelevant. This has nothing to do with the will in question."

Judge Griffin said, "Objection overruled. You will answer the question, Mr. Black."

"I, yes, I am aware that the property is in litigation."

"And you, Mr. Black, assuming that you are a business man, what kind of business are you engaged in?"

"I have a furniture store in Baton Rogue."

"Very well. And do you have a family?"

"Objection, your honor. What does that have to do with the will in question?"

"Sustained. Continue, Mr. Winfield."

"Mr. Black, this property, the Jackson Estate, that is in litigation . . . is it not true that the National State Bank in Baton Rogue is in a lawsuit about money that was borrowed against this property? Are you aware of that?"

"Yes, I am."

"And Mr. Black, aren't you a member of the board of directors at that bank?"

"Objection your honor."

"Overruled. Answer the question."

"Aren't you a member on the board of directors of that bank?"

"I am."

"And so, if that bank wins this lawsuit and possesses this property, then you will benefit."

"Objection, your honor."

"Overruled. Answer the questions."

"Give me an answer, yes or no."

"Yes."

"And meanwhile if Mrs. Jackson wins the lawsuit you will stand to benefit on that side also because she would want to at least honor your work by giving you some type of honorarium."

"I cannot say that she would do that," Mr. Black said.

"Anyway, however it turns out, it's like burning both ends

of the candle. You stand to benefit whomever gets it. Am I correct?"

"That is what you say."

"Mr. Black, have you ever had an alias?"

"I beg your pardon?"

"Have you ever had a name other than Thomas Jefferson Black?"

"Why should I?"

"Sir, is it not true that one of the reasons that the Jackson Estate is in litigation is because in his will Mr. Jackson included two children he fathered out of wedlock?"

Mr. Black looked surprised. He retorted and said, "They are both dead and neither one has any children."

"No more questions, your honor."

"You may step down, Mr. Black. Lawyer Glass you may call your second witness."

"I have no other witnesses, your honor."

"Then Mr. Winfield you may call your first witness."

"I call Professor Allen Love."

Professor Love went up, took the oath, gave his name, and sat down. Chester Winfield proceeded to question him.

"Professor Love, did you know Miss Millie Stone?"

"Yes sir, I did."

"About how long have you known her?"

"I taught in this community for four years, and since that time I frequently visited many friends who I knew while teaching here. Miss Stone, or Aunt Millipus, was one of those people."

"I understand that you were instrumental in helping Miss Stone make out her will. Is that correct?"

"That is correct."

"Please tell us how this came about."

"Well, the last year that I taught here in this community at Crossroads, Miss Stone sent for me and wanted me to help advise her about how to make out her will."

"I suppose that you did go."

"I did go."

"Did you go alone?"

"I did not."

"Who went with you?"

"Mr. Jason Winfield."

"Were there any other people with you beside you two?"

"No, we were the only people with her."

"And why did she have Jason come with you?"

"Miss Stone was a very smart, very religious person with high morals. She did not want me in her house unless someone else was there. She did not want my wife to be burdened with my problem, and since Jason had become just like a son that she never had at this age, she wanted him to be present when I gave her the advice."

"And did she say to you that she wanted to make the will out to Jason?"

"She did not."

"Did she tell you how she came about this property?"

"She did."

"And what did she say?"

"She said that when she was living in Louisiana she had two children by her slave master, George Jackson, and since he knew that they were his, she said that one day he took her upstairs in his private office and told her that he had been to Texas and had bought and paid for two hundred acres of land for her and those two children."

"And did she say what happened?"

"She said that he told her that he had made out the will and told her where he was going to put it. He gave her a key to the trunk and the attic where the will would be and that she was no more a slave. He also said that he had a heart condition and wanted these two children he had fathered by her to have a home because the four thousand-acre plantations, the Jackson Estate, was enough for his wife and their son. And after a short time Millie Stone and one of the servants named Uncle Aaron were out in the yard, and they heard a gunshot. She was a much faster runner than Uncle Aaron, so she beat him upstairs. She found Colonel Jackson dead. She picked up the gun and gave it to Uncle Aaron. There were those who wanted to believe that she killed Colonel Jackson in order to get away from the plantation. She stayed on for awhile to help with Mrs. Jackson, who had broken her back riding a horse. Mrs. Jackson's brother came to run the plantation. Millie's son, who was seventeen, and Mrs. Jackson's brother, Jeff Stanley, got into an altercation. They sent the son away lest Mr. Stanley would have him killed. She and her daughter went away to New Orleans, and her daughter died. Mrs. Stone came to Texas. The report came to her about her son being drowned in Louisiana. She ended up in

Texas. She met the Winfield family here in Texas and got a job housekeeping for the Webb family."

"Jason was there when she told you the story?"

"Yes, he was. She did not say anything about willing the property to Jason that day. She wanted my advice about how to make out a will."

"What happened later?"

"Well, later on—a few years later—I came out here to a celebration, and she told me she was ready to make out her will. I took her back to the city with me and got a lawyer, and she made out the will."

"And to whom did you deed the two hundred acres?"

"She said she wanted to deed it to Jason Winfield. The other contents of the house and the horse and the cow were given to other people, including the churches in the community."

"And what did she do with the deeds?"

"She placed one in the safe deposit box in the bank here in Koohne Town. She gave me a copy, and she took a copy and told me that she was going to put it in her trunk and lock up the trunk. And if she passed on she wanted me to be the administrator of the will."

"Thank you, Professor Love. Your witness, Mr. Glass."

Lawyer Glass stepped forward. "Mr. Love, you said that Miss Stone, Aunt Millipus as y'all would say this, was an honest person? How would you determine this?"

"Well, she often visited the school where I was teaching, and she was a constant attendee at the church. She shared what she had with so many people."

"And you say that when she sent for you to give her advice about making this, that she did not mention anyone she wanted to make it to?"

"At that time it seemed that she was undecided because she had befriended many people in the community. She was not ready to make the will. She only wanted to know how to go about doing it."

"Professor Love, it seems to me that even though there was a difference in your ages you were quite friendly with Jason Winfield. Would you explain this to me?"

"Well, I had taught Jason for four years in school. He was a very intelligent young man. He made good grades, had good manners, and because of his demeanor, I felt like the young

117

man had a chance of becoming a very intellectual business and professional person if he had a chance to finish his education. I understood that his parents were not able to send him to college. So my wife Geraldine and I found a college in the city where he could work his way through the school. I talked to his parents about this, and we just wanted to help him."

"Did this Jason go to school?" Lawyer Glass asked.

"No, he did not. His father was killed, and he had to assume the responsibility of his family, his mother, sisters, and brothers."

"I see. Of all of the young men in the community you took a special interest in Jason over all of the other boys that were going to school."

"I took an interest in Jason because of his family's financial situation at that time and because of his aggressive spirit at that time. I was interested in all of the boys, but Jason seemed like the kind of boy who would go far in life."

"So then ya'll are good friends and because Miss Stone entrusted you to help her with this will would you say that Jason Winfield would profit by Aunt Millipus' death if you encouraged her to make the will out to him?"

"Objection, Your honor."

"Sustained. Go ahead."

"Mr. Love, when did Miss Stone tell you that she wanted Jason to be the beneficiary of this two hundred acres of land?"

"She told me that when I took her back home with me, and I helped her make out the will."

"Are you sure that Jason did not know anything about this?" the lawyer asked.

"I am sure that I didn't tell him, and I don't think Miss Stone told him."

"Mr. Love, why did Miss Stone make a choice of you to do all of this for her when she had others she could have chosen from?"

"I thought I explained that as best I could. The best person to have asked would have been Miss Stone, and unfortunately she is not here to answer that question. Whatever her choice was I just merely did what she asked me to do."

"Do you feel that you would be benefited in a monetary way by Aunt Millipus making this will to Jason?"

"Sir, I think if Aunt Millipus would have wanted me to benefit by this she had plenty of chances to have said so. She could have even put me in her will for that matter. I humbly submit to you that it would be impossible for me to have read her mind. I sure can't read it now, and if you have other questions that you would want answered, if you have any kind of super powers then you might want to get in touch with Aunt Millipus and let her answer these questions."

There was a snickering in the audience.

Lawyer Glass asked, "Have I insulted you by these questions? If so, I am sorry. No more questions."

The judge said, "You may step down Mr. Love. You may call your next witness, Mr. Winfield."

Lawyer Chester Winfield said, "I call Mr. Jason Winfield."

Jason mounted the stand and took the oath. The judge said, "Will you state your name?"

"Jason Winfield"

"You may proceed."

"Jason, how long have you known Aunt Millipus or Miss Stone as presented?"

"I have known her, sir, since I was a very small boy."

"Did you do services for her?"

"Yes, I did."

"And what were some of those services?"

"Well, after she took up residence on the small place, I assisted her with chores around the house, such as chopping wood for her fireplace and cook stove. I was there to carry the wood into the house, help her with her gardening, and run errands for her."

"And when she began to be in bad health, did you continue to do this?"

"Yes sir, I did."

"Were you paid to do this?"

"When I was smaller and younger, she gave me change at times or little things to eat, but after I had gotten to be in my teens I would not accept her money. I did accept her cooking." There were a few laughs at that remark.

"And you did know that Miss Stone planned to make a will, is that correct?"

"I did, yes sir, I did."

"And would you like to tell us how that came about?"

"Yes sir. Aunt Millipus . . . when I was about seventeen years old and was planning to go to the city to college, she told me to tell Professor Love, who was my teacher, that she wanted him to come to her house to visit with her and to instruct her on how to make a will. She told me to come with him."

"And, of course, you did as she told you."

"Yes, I did."

"And briefly tell us what she told you and Professor Love that day."

"She told us her life story and as pertaining to this part of the will about the land she told us that it was given to her by her former slave master for her and her two children. As far as she knew they both were dead she planned to give this land to some acquaintance."

"And did she say who she was going to make the will to?"

"She said she had not decided . . . . she only wanted to know the procedure."

"Did she mention your name as a prospect?"

"No sir, she did not."

"Jason, I understand that you found Miss Stone dead in her house. Would you like to tell us about that?"

"Yes sir, I had keys to her house because she trusted me. But I never used the keys unless it was an occasion when she was not at home and I had to do things for her. But when she was at home, I always knocked and she would come to the door and admit me. When her health began to fail, I visited her everyday. If I didn't go in the morning, I would go and see her I would go to bed at night. She was never a bed patient. She still cooked for herself and kept her house and even occasionally still did service as a midwife. But on this particular morning, I knocked several times and she did not answer. Then I banged on the door and shouted her name and still no answer. So I became anxious. I took my key to her house and unlocked the door and went in. I found her on her bed. She was dead. This was a new experience for me. It was as if I was dreaming. I called her name. I touched her to try to shake her, but her body was cold and stiff and I knew that she was dead."

"And then what did you do?"

"I closed the door, locked it, and went over to the Randolph's house. I told Mr. and Mrs. Randolph what had happened, gave them the key, and asked them if they would go over there and get Mose to go and get my mother while I went to Koohne Town to get the Justice of Peace so that he could verify her death. I asked them not to bother the body until I got back with the investigator."

"And the justice of peace did go back with you?"

"Yes sir, he did."

"And how did you go to Koohne Town."

"I rode my horse."

"And what was the justice of peace's verdict?"

"He said from all indications she died from natural cause."

"Jason, when did you become aware that Miss Stone had put you in her will?"

"It was only after Professor Love had notified all of the people whom she had put in the will as her beneficiaries."

"Did she ever tell you that she was thinking about putting you in the will?"

"No sir, not ever."

"No more questions your honor."

The judge said to the plaintiff, "You may cross examine the witness."

Lawyer Glass came forward folding then unfolding his arms. He asked, "Jason, you said you have known Miss Millipus for most of your life."

"Yes sir, that is correct."

"You heard and knew about the land that was deeded to her in deep East Texas."

"Yes sir, I did."

"And who read the deeds that day when you said that Aunt Millipus sent for you to come over?"

"Profosser Love read the deeds."

"In your presence?"

"Yes, sir."

"And how old did you say you were?"

"Seventeen."

"And did you know anything about deed and legal actions?"

"No more than I had learned in school under Professor Love's teaching."

"Did you understand that the land was to go back to the owner if there was no immediate offsprings of this family?"

"Sir, the deed did not say go back to the owner; it said back to the Jackson Estate."

"Since her children were dead and she had no other children, did you understand that that meant the property would go back to be a part of the Jackson Estate in Louisiana?"

"Yes sir, I did understand that."

"Jason, I heard you say a few minutes ago that it was you who found Aunt Millipus dead."

"Yes, sir."

"Did you know at the time that she died that she had made a will?"

"No sir, I did not."

"You mean to tell me that this woman who had almost but adopted you, who had taken you into her confidence and let you know her business and her affairs all of these years had not told you about the deed? You had seen the deeds . . . you had heard them read . . . . and yet after all of your going to see her every-day she never told you that she had made out her will?"

"Sir, she never told me, and I never asked her."

"I understand that you have a small lumber mill. Is that correct?"

"Yes sir, I do."

"And you cut down trees and make lumber?"

"That is correct."

"Does the land belong to you?"

"That is correct."

"And since you are in the business of cutting trees and making lumber, as I understand it, there are many pine trees on this land that we are discussing and it stands to reason that you would be benefited by being included in this will. Am I right?"

Chester Winfield, said, "Objection your honor."

"Sustained," the judge said.

"Well, since everybody knew that Miss Stone was sick, her death could not be such a shock to the people in the community. Wouldn't you say? Most people knew that she was sick, but it seems to me that if anybody knew that she was sick that you would be more familiar about her sickness than most people. Am I right?"

"Your honor, these persons have no bearing on the deed."

"Objection."

"We are talking about a deed, but we are also talking about life and death. I think Jason should answer the question."

"Sustained."

"You may answer the question, Jason."

"I knew that Aunt Millie was sick; I knew that she was tak-ing medicine and I knew that her health was failing. But I think you will have to understand that when you walk into her room and find somebody dead that you had just talked to the day be-

122

fore, who seems to be doing all right in her case, that it is shocking."

"And nobody else was there when you found her dead?"

"No, sir."

"So we only have your word that she was dead when you entered the house"

"That is correct."

"And did the justice of peace ascertain how long she had been dead?"

"Yes, he said she had been dead for probably several hours."

"But by the time you got over your shock, locked the door, went to the Randolph's house, told them what happened, gave them the keys, went to Koohne Town which was four to five miles, found the justice of the peace, waited for him to get ready, saddled his horse, and came back it will only seem natural that her body would have been cold by that time."

"Sir, I found the body cold."

"That is your word Jason, but you will admit that you would benefit by the death of Aunt Millie."

"I did not know what was in the will."

"So you say. But now we all know that somebody else knew that you were in the will and that somebody else could have told you. With those big hands of yours you could easily have put her to sleep forever and told people you found her dead."

"Objection, your honor."

Chester Winfield was on the floor. "This is ridiculous. This man has the audacity to stand here and insinuate that Jason, who loved this old lady like his own mother and who was terribly hurt by her death, could killed her."

"Objection sustained."

"No more questions, your honor."

"Jason, you may step down." The judge said to the plaintiff, "You may have your final summation."

Lawyer Glass came forward. "Your honor, we have before us today, as has been presented, the story of a woman who had proof that a George Jackson willed her and her children some land in Texas. He showed her the deed; told her where he put them; gave her the keys to where they were; and less than a month later this man is found by the benefactor, so she says, shot to death. When one of the workers on the farm went up the stairs and entered the room, he found Aunt Millipus, the benefactor, with the gun in her hand and George Jackson dead. Now why would she have the gun in her hand and then say that he killed himself? With his death she could now claim the 200 acres of land and stay around for a few days as if she were mourning her loss, and then within weeks take a fly-by-night exit and nobody would know where she had gone until months and months later where she shows up in Texas. But who was to benefit by the man's death?—Millipus Stone. She took the will and kept it, and instead of just claiming the land and even living there if she wanted to, she came to this town. For whatever reason, I don't know, she seems to have fallen in love with some young man and after a time decided to will him this property. Now Mr. Chester Winfield has suggested that since the deed did not name George Jackson as the person who purchased the land, he would be the recipient or could reclaim the land if she and her children passed on and there were no immediate relatives. And because it is said, possibly in error, it did not say 'back to George Jackson' but 'back to the Jackson Quarters' that the said name would not be entitled to this property. I think Mr. Winfield and all of my listeners would hopefully agree that we are dealing with the intent of the statement rather than looking so hard at the word 'Jackson Quarters.' We need to look at the intent. Now Miss Stone . . . we are not questioning the will that she made out. That was her prerogative. But we do have to question her death and consider that the beneficiary of this land in the will was the only one who found her dead, so he said, and we have only his word. I would like to conclude that we have two peculiar deaths in these episodes, both, of which I suggest, are strange. I would further suggest that in both cases it would have been murder. And so when we look at all of these things, I submit to you that the deeds are invalid and that the property should go back to the Jackson Quarters. Thank you, your Honor."

"Lawyer Winfield, you may present your final argument."

Chester Winfield came forward with papers in his hands. "Your Honor, I am here to represent a young man by the name of Jason Winfield. I have known him all of my life. A man of integrity with strong religious convictions; a fine citizen of the community; a hard working man who has never had a run-in with the law for any reason. Jason is a man about whom most anyone in this community would verify what I am saying. To accuse this man of being a murderer is not only an insult to his integrity but also an insult to this whole town and country where the effect of his life is felt. We've all heard what the coroner has said about Miss Stone's death.

"Now concerning the deed, Mr. Glass has suggested that we should look at the intent rather than the words. How can you read the intent when we have it in black and white—that the land would go back to the Jackson Quarters when it never was a part of the Jackson Quarters? How can you go back to where you have never been? If I might suggest that is why our Lord Jesus Christ, many of you know him in this room, (there were soft amens heard in the audience) he did not go to the dirt when he died because he did not come from the dust. He could not go where he did not come from. His body came from heaven and he went back to heaven."

On the side where the black folks were sitting there were many amens, hallelujahs, and thanks you God's.

Lawyer Winfield continued, "All I am saying is that I believe, if I may borrow Mr. Glass' own words, that maybe Mr. Jackson knew what he was doing when he added the words 'back to the quarters' in the deed. He probably knew that the land did not come from the quarters and that the particular phrase was put in there so that nobody who came to occupy the Jackson Quarters at that time could claim the land. Perhaps Miss Stone could see that. This being so, if the will does not stand, then what is going to happen to the land considering these things I have pointed out? The only other thing I know would be that the land would go to the county or to the state of Texas who has more land that any state in the union. In closing, I submit that your honor let the will stand as read. Thank you."

The judge said, "I will go to my chambers for a few minutes and ponder the case of these witnesses. Then I'll come back in about twenty minutes and give you my verdict."

At that moment Victoria Webb, who was sitting with her parents and a man who was a stranger in that town, rose up and went to Chester Winfield and said something to him.

Then Chester Winfield said to the Judge, "Your honor, I have a surprise witness who would like to testify for the defense if you will grant it."

Lawyer Glass was immediately on the floor. "Your honor, Mr. Winfield has had his chance and he just said a few minutes ago, 'No more witnesses.' I think you should rule out any more people who may want to testify."

Chester Winfield replied, "Your Honor, I feel that this witness may have some information that has not been presented. I would want you to grant her that privilege of giving her testimony."

Judge Griffin said, "Very well counselor, the witness may come forward."

Victoria came forward dressed in a very becoming soft pink dress. She took the stand. The judge swore her in and said, "Would you give your name?"

She replied, "Victoria Webb."

"You may take your seat and proceed with your testimony."

"I thought I could keep silent in this case that is being presented, but I feel that it would be a coward act if I did not speak on behalf of the benefactor in person. I could not sit there and have the personality of such a noble person butchered by people who possibly don't know who she really was. Since she is in her grave and cannot defend her character, I had no choice but to come forward and give this testimony. I have known Miss Stone, or Aunt Millipus as she was frequently called, practically all of my life. She came to work for my parents when I was less than three years old. My mother, Marie Webb, had decided to go into the classroom and be an instructor at the Koohne High School, and she was looking for someone to be a nursemaid for me and a general housekeeper. Through the Randolph family she was able to make the acquaintance of Aunt Millipus, who was living with them at the time and doing day work in the fields. Mrs. Randolph highly recommended her and, as a result, my parents moved her into the servants quarters and gave her the jobs of taking care of me, keeping the house, and cooking our meals. She was an excellent cook. She was faithful to work whenever she was needed—day or night. And the only time that she requested off were two Sundays in the month—every other Sunday to attend her church services. She was a very religious person.

"When I was eighteen years old I finished high school, and by that time Aunt Millipus had begun to have rheumatism in her legs and had a problem going up and down the stairs in the house. She told my parents that she was ready to retire and that since I would be going to college, they could go on and hire somebody else to do the job that she had been doing. My parents tried hard to persuade her to keep on working and told her that she would not even have to climb the stairs when she didn't

126

feel like it. But she argued that it would not be right for her to take money from them when she could not do her job as the duty called for. So in the end, with some regrets, my parents gave in to her wishes.

"They bought her an acre and a half of land up at the crossroads and bought her a two-room house from Koohne Town. The colored men in the community moved the house for free. They built her a chimney and a flute for her kitchen. They dug her a well, and my parents gave her furniture out of the servants quarters so she would not need to purchase anything but a cook stove. They told her that if she would come to work for them a couple of days a week whenever she felt like it they would keep her on the payroll. This allowed her to do her gardening with a horse that we had given her and a little buggy given to her by from grown children from a colored couple who had died. She used the horse, sometimes riding it and other times hitching it to the buggy, and went through the community and other communities where she did midwife service for women who were having babies. She also sold vegetables out of her garden as well as made cookies and other little goodies, which she would sell at picnics or other public affairs in the community. I still frequently visited her because I enjoyed her cooking so much.

"When I was a senior in college, I came for the Christmas holidays and as usual I went to see her. She had already sent word by one of our field workers that she wanted me to come and eat breakfast with her because she wanted to talk to me and wanted me to give her some advice. I went to see her Monday after Christmas and, sure enough, she had my breakfast ready. We sat down and ate together and then she told me to just leave everything as it is on the table and for us go into the bedroom and talk. There was something in her voice that aroused my anxiety, and I wondered if she was having some kind of problem or if her sickness gotten worse.

"It was a cold day. A stiff northern was blowing outside. She placed some more wood on the fireplace, and it was very comfortable in the room as she sat in her favorite rocking chair and I sat in the other . . . both of us facing the fireplace.

"She said, 'This is quite a long story. I want to tell you the history of my life.' She told the story for the most part that she had told to Professor Love and Jason. And then she told me about her getting a job working at the saloon and eating place

127

in New Orleans and her daughter getting a job taking in washing and ironing for a white family. She also told me that while they were living in New Orleans that her daughter, Jeannie Mae, had a child by a white man and that she was very upset when she found out that Jeannie Mae was pregnant. Aunt Millie had built up a bitterness in her heart against white people for all that she had gone through. But surprisingly, when the baby was born, Aunt Millie loved the little baby although she tried to hide her affection from her daughter.

"When Jeannie Mae was not around, she would follow the baby, kiss it, powder it, and just hold the baby in her arms and all up in her chest. She decided that nobody was ever going to take this baby away from her, if she could help it. In case they did, and because the baby was completely white, Aunt Millipus did not want anybody, for any reason, to come and claim this white baby. But in case they did, she decided to have an 'x' tattooed on the baby's left thigh, and then she had the same person to tattoo an 'x' on her thigh in exactly the same place in the same way. If the baby was ever taken away from her, she would then be able to find it by the 'x'.

"One night Aunt Millipus came home and found that Jeannie Mae and the baby were gone. She told how she could not find Jeannie Mae or her child and how a year later Jeannie Mae came back home without the baby. She finally told about what she did after burying her daughter and what she decided to do to try to find the baby on the little information that she had.

"Aunt Millipus said, 'I came to Texas and I found my grandchild with the information that my daughter had given me. I could not be absolutely certain, but when I saw the child I realized that this had to be my grandchild.'

"She said to me, 'The child was with a very wealthy family, was well taken care of in a fine home, and had everything a little child would want. So I felt like the child would be better off with this family, who could do so much more for her than I could. And since the family was white and the child looked as white as they were, if not whiter, I decided to let her alone as long as I knew where the child was. So now that the child is grown and I still have the deed to the two hundred and a half acres of property that Colonel George gave to me and my children . . . and since my daughter is dead and my son they say got drowned, I only have this grandchild as a family member . . .

and since I am getting old and I know I won't be around much longer, I want to will this 200 acres of land to my grandchild. But then the child would know, and the parents would know and all of the friends would know that she had a colored grandma. Now, I told you I wanted your opinion about the will. Should I make this will out to my grandchild?'

"I said to Aunt Millipus, 'I need to ask you a question. Is this a boy or a girl?'

"And she said to me, 'It's a girl.'

"So I asked, 'And you say you know where she is?'

"And Aunt Millipus said, 'Yes, I do.'

"I asked, 'Would I be asking too much if I asked you where this girl is?'"

"To which she replied, 'I am talking to her. Victoria you are my grandchild.'

There was a buzz that went through the audience . . . ohhh and aahhs. "She said, 'I am Aunt Millipus' grandchild. And when I heard all of these innuendoes and accusations about the integrity of this woman who helped so many and could not defend herself, I am here to tell you that most anybody who knew her would tell you that she was an honest, kind, and loving Christian woman. I need not tell you, you can imagine, how shocked I was. And I said to her, 'Aunt Millipus, are you sure of this?'

"She got up out of her chair and went to a little trunk in the corner of her bedroom. She took a key from around her neck, unlocked the trunk, and got a little black Bible out of it and gave it to me. She showed me where she had recorded the date of birth of her two children, the date of her mother's death, the date of my birth, and the date of my mother's death.

"She said to me, 'Your real name is Queen Victoria Jackson. You were such a pretty baby that we called you Queen Victoria. You will see that right here in the Bible.'

"She went and got a brown envelope and took out some pictures of my mother, her brother Johnie, and a picture of my mother, her brother and herself. There were pictures of the children, and Colonel George, their father.

"He had taken all of them to town and had these pictures made and she said, 'I am going to give you a picture of your mother, your grandfather, and your uncle. I am going to give you one of you and your mother. I will keep the rest. You need not tell anyone about who they are because no one knows anyhow. But I wanted you to have them.'

129

"And then she showed me the deeds to this 200 acres of land. She showed me my mother's wedding and engagement ring and a beautiful necklace that was my mother's wedding present from her husband. It had some small diamonds in it too. She gave it to me for my Christmas present, and I'm wearing it today. But back to our conversation.

"Aunt Millipus said, 'Now that you know the whole truth, do you want me to will you this land?'

"To this I hardly knew what to say because if my family and my friends found out that I had Negro blood in me I would probably be rejected. I didn't know what to say. I wondered why Aunt Millipus came and found me; why she didn't just leave things as they were. I loved her, but when I thought about what I would have to give up I said, 'Well, Aunt Millie, let me think about this. It is so sudden, I guess I am in shock.' I did not want to hurt her feelings. She showed me the 'x' on her thigh just like the one on mine, and I knew she had to be telling the truth. Since she was my only true relative would it be right for me to deny my ancestry?

"She said, 'If you don't want it to be, I'll just hush my mouth.'

"I asked her if she had told anybody else in Koohne Town or Crossroads what she had told me. And she told me that she had told two people that swore that they would tell no one unless I said to; they were Professor Love and Jason. She said she had not told another soul.

"I said to her, 'Let me think about it and when I come back home for Easter, I'll give you my answer.'

"I took the necklace and the pictures; got up out of the chair, kissed her, and walked out of her house that cold winter afternoon. I walked with a heavy heart. I did not have the spirit to even get off the horse that I was riding back to the house. I was so puzzled and perplexed and I might say even sad. It was a bad Christmas for me. I lost my appetite.

"Trey Koohne, whom I had been dating since my first year in college, could not deal with my moods. Even my parents were disturbed about the change in my attitude and I could not tell them what the problem was. I was glad to go back to college . . . away from Trey, away from my family, and even away from Aunt Millipus and try to work this thing out.

"By the time Easter came, I had made up my mind and my decision was that I could not with a clear conscious deny my relationship with my real grandmother. So the Saturday before Easter I went to visit her and told her that I had considered it, and my final decision was that I did not particularly care about accepting the will for the land, but my decision was to let it be known that she was my real grandmother. I also suggested to her that since Jason had been like a son to her and had seen after her all of these years that I would be satisfied if she willed Jason the two hundred and a half acres of land.

"To this she replied, 'Victoria, I told you I was going to pray over this. And I think the Lord has answered my prayers. Early one morning before day, the answer came to me just as if somebody was speaking to me.' And this is what it said, 'Millie, deed the land to your granddaughter and deed it in her original name—Queen Victoria Jackson—because nobody knows you by this name. After the deeds have been completed and notarized you should buy the land back from Queen Jackson and then it is no longer Jackson property. It would be Millie Stone's property. Then you can will the property to anybody you want to. You can go to some other county if you do not want to do it here and nobody will ever know the difference. Now what do you think about this because I believe the Lord revealed this to me. You can still have the Webbs for your parents, and you can still marry Richard III and you can still have your job at the school, and nobody but you, Jason, and Professor Love will know the whole story.'

"I felt badly because I felt she was trying to protect me and I told her so. However, she insisted, so in the end we agreed with her plan. She deeded the land to me under the original name—Queen Victoria Jackson. This was all done secretly. When it was all finished she gave me an envelope with ten twenty dollar bills in it which was the amount that we agreed the land would be exchanged for. I wrote her a receipt for the money but would not take the actual money.

"We almost argued about that but she said to me, 'I am going to tell you what ole man Jackson used to say—A deal is a deal.' Aunt Millipus still refused to take the money. So when everything was completed I took the deeds and the receipts and put them in an envelope and without her knowing it I put the $200 in the envelope with the deeds. I put an extra $100 in it for her. I replaced the ten twenty dollar bills with two $100 dollar bills and I sealed the envelope up.

"I was home for a week, and she sent for me to come back

the following Wednesday. She told me she had something she wanted me to help her do. She said, 'I am going to go ahead and will the 200 acres of land to Jason Winfield and I'm going to will this place and everything I have with the exception of my jewelry and my trunk—your mother's things—to my friends in the community. I want you to have your mother's jewelry and the trunk. When Professor Love comes down for the 19th of June celebration, I am going back to the city with him and he is going to carry me to a lawyer and make the will.'

"Professor Love did come down in June and I was back home from school—I had finished college—and she did go back to the city with Professor Love. She made the will about a week after she came back from the city. She sent for me again and she said, 'I want you to help me do something.'

"What she wanted was for me to help her to put a false bottom in her trunk. She had a handsaw and some apple boxes, which we tore up. We measured the length and width of the inside of the trunk and cut pieces of the box that fit firmly at the bottom. Then she went and got the original deeds that Colonel Jackson had given her, the deeds that I had deeded to her, and the copy of her will, and put it in the bottom of the trunk. She placed the sealed envelope that I sealed with the money in it. She had never opened it. It was sealed and put in the bottom of the trunk. We took the pieces of the apple box that had been finished, placed them in the trunk, took some candy tacks, and nailed the apple box to the bottom of the trunk. Then she took some velvet cloth and together we glued the cloth to the apple boxes.

"Then she said to me, 'Now you know where the deeds are—the first one where I got the land from Colonel Jackson, the one where I deeded it to Victoria, the one where I bought it back from Victoria, and a copy of her will.'

"Again she said, 'I want you to have my trunk. It is in my will and nobody will suspect that you are my granddaughter. Now I can go to my grave knowing that I have done my best for the only person in this world that I know I have as a part of my body.'

"Your honor, I have the trunk outside in the wagon. Would you permit me to bring it in as evidence?"

The judge said, "Yes."

Lawyer Glass was on his feet, "Objection your Honor, I don't think this is necessary."

The judge said, "Overruled. If this has some evidence pertaining to this case, it needs to be permitted."

Two young men brought the little trunk into the courtroom. Victoria gave a key to the judge and explained that the trunk had been kept in the Randolph store at his request until today. She asked the judge to unlock the trunk, remove the tray, and pry the false bottoms out.

The judge obliged by taking a knife and a screwdriver and prying the false bottom up. Sure enough there were all the envelopes that Aunt Millipus had placed some two or three years before. The jewelry was in a small cookbook that had to be removed before he could pry the false bottom out. The judge examined the original deed by Colonel Jackson and then he examined the deeds that he had made and deeded to Aunt Millipus. Then he opened the sealed envelope and the deed that Victoria made to her for her purchasing the land. The receipt was still there. The audience was amazed when the judge pulled out the three one hundred-dollar bills and showed them to the audience.

The judge also opened the envelope with the will in it and then he said, "It is all here, Miss Webb, just as you said." The judge read the will so that all could hear. He said:

LAST WILL AND TESTAMENT
State of Texas
Be it known by all men present
That I, Emily Stone, of Koohne Town, TX
Being of sound and dispositioned mind and memory, do hereby make my will and testament, hereby revoking all wills heretofore made by me. I direct that my just debts be paid. My estate will be distributed as follows:
To the churches I leave $50.00 each, which should to be used to buy a new pulpit and chairs;
To Buck and Lucinda Jones I will my milk cow;
To Mose and Ellie Randolph I will my horse;
To Victoria Webb I will all of my jewelry, my trunk, and a key to the trunk;
To Jason and Violet Winfield I will my acre and a half of land, my house and everything in it, except the items for Victoria, and two hundred acres of land in Cherokee County, Texas.

Executed the 24th day of June 1897.

133

The judge continued, "I think I will take a short recess and come back in thirty minutes. Then I will give you my decision. Is that the end of your testimony, Miss Webb?"

"No," she said to the judge. "That's not quite the end. I have something else I need to say before you make your decision."

"You may speak," he said.

She said, "Your honor, even though I sincerely believe Aunt Millipus' story, after this lawsuit came up, I really wanted to completely satisfy myself. So I bought a train ticket to New Orleans. I had told my family I just wanted to go away for a while. I had to show myself without a doubt that what Aunt Millipus had told me was true. I went to the courthouse and surveyed records and found the copy of Queen Victoria Jackson's birth certificate. I found the death certificate of my mother, Jeannie Mae Jackson. I inquired until I found the cemetery where my mother was buried. I went to that cemetery and found a small stone that listed her name, her birthdate, and the day she died. The epitaph said, "Gone but not forgotten." I left New Orleans and went to a small town up the river and inquired about Jackson Quarters. When I found out where it was, I hired a man, hackney, to take me to that plantation early one morning.

"When I got there I saw a row of houses, most of which were log cabins, and I asked some children who where playing if they knew an old gentleman named Uncle Aaron. They showed me where he lived. The man drove me to the cabin. They parked the carriage under the tree. I got out at the gate that was a part of the fence that was around the house.

"An old colored man was sitting on the porch in his chair. I called from the gate, 'Are you Uncle Aaron Jackson?' He answered, 'Yes.' I continued, 'Could I come and talk to you for a while?'"

"'Yes ma'am. Just unhook the gate and come in,' he replied. I opened the gate and walked down the little brick walk that they had made. Flowers were blooming on either side of the walk. The fragrance was in my nostrils. The flowers were growing and blooming in a profusion of rainbow colors. I don't believe there was a weed among any of them. On the westside of the porch there was a network of colors. There was a row of morning glories, which was running on strings and completely shaded the area. Since it was mid-morning the vines were in full purple blossoms. On the east side of the porch I observed that there was a shelf running the length of that side and on it and on the shelf were pans filled with moss, which were in full bloom.

"At his invitation I stepped up on the porch. I said, 'Oh, your flowers are beautiful.'

"'Thank you,' he replied without moving. The chair I discovered had been made out of willows and it was in a reclining position. He had a walking cane across his lap. I said, 'I hope you don't mind, I just came to ask you a few questions.'

"He looked at me suspiciously. Then he said, 'Lady, what do you want to ask me?' I could tell that he assumed that I was a white woman and he didn't seem to be very anxious to talk to me. Again he asked, 'What do you want to ask me?'

"I replied, 'I want to ask you some questions about a woman who used to live on this plantation.'

"'Well lady,' he replied, 'there have been a lot of women who lived on this plantation, years and years. Some been dead and gone. What's the woman's name?'

"I replied, 'Millipus Stone or better known as Millipus.'

"His face immediately lighted up and he said, 'Lady I ain't heard from that woman in over twenty some odd years.'

"I said to him, 'I am Aunt Millipus' granddaughter.'

"To which he replied, 'What?'

"I'll repeat it," I said, "I am Aunt Millipus' granddaughter. Aunt Millipus had two children. Her son was named Johnie and her daughter was named Jeannie Mae."

"He said, 'You're right, you're right. Where is Aunt Millipus?'

"I said, 'She's dead.'

"He said, 'Woman you go away from here. You say you are her granddaughter?'

"I said, 'Yes, Jeannie Mae was my mommy.'

"'And where is Jeannie Mae?' he asked.

"She's dead too," I said.

"He answered, 'Woman, hush you mouth.' He hollered to his wife, 'Come here.' His wife had been listening behind the door and came out. He said, 'This woman claims she is Aunt Millipus' granddaughter.' She replied, 'Lord have mercy.'

"I went into my purse and brought out some pictures and showed them to Uncle Aaron and his wife. I showed them the picture of my mother and Uncle Johnie together, a picture of Col. George Jackson and my mother and uncle together, and a picture of Aunt Millipus and her two children together.

"They looked at all of the pictures and said, 'Lord have mercy, here's Aunt Millipus. She was a pretty girl she was. She had pretty eyes, pretty hair, and pretty legs.' Without batting an eye he said, 'and pretty titties.'

"'And you say that she is dead? I haven't heard from her since she left. And now where are you from?' I said, 'I am from Texas.'

"Let me ask you something? I said, Did you ever hear anything from my Uncle Johnie? My grandmother told me that you helped them escape from possibly being killed because he had a fight with a white man.

"'Woman,' he said, 'You sho' telling the truth. I did I told him since he looked white he would be better off if he told everybody that he was a white man. I told him that when I opened this plantation. I said to him that night, if you turn white don't you ever forget that you are a colored man. Don't ever forget it.'

"He continued, 'When I got back here, Aunt Millipus and Jeannie had left on one of the horses that Colonel George gave to them. I ain't seen nor heard from them to this day.'

"I said, 'Have you heard from Johnie since?'

"'Yes ma'am,' he said. 'He came here about two years after he ran away. Late one night while looking for his momma and sister. I told him I didn't know what had happened to them.'

"Uncle Aaron sat there feeling on his walking stick, and I sat on a chair that had been given to me. I positioned myself so that I could see him while he talked. He explained that Johnie came back here about two or three years ago. He was a white man, dressed fine and he hardly knew him. Johnie told us he was living in a place called Cincinnati, Ohio. He said he was selling land. He was a white man, but he said to me, 'I ain't never forgot what you told to me. I am still a colored man.'

"He gave my wife and me some money. He gave us a self-addressed envelope. He also told us to contact him if we ever heard anything from his family. We were to send back the envelope so that he would know about them.

"Victoria asked for his address since the Jacksons were no longer there anymore. He said to me, 'I'll give you the address.' He hollered to his wife, 'Hon, look in that Bible and get the address so that I can give it to the lady.' Uncle Aaron made a copy of the address on the envelope and then gave it to me.

"Then I said to him, 'Uncle Aaron, what did Johnie and a white man have a fight about?'

"He looked at his wife who was still standing in the door and said, 'Tell her honey.' She said to me, 'do you really want to know?' To which I replied, 'Yes ma'am I really want to know.'

"'Well, I'll tell you,' she said. She pulled up a bench and turned the bench so that she was facing me. She continued, 'They had a fight because he raped your momma and Johnie jumped on him. He cut Johnie behind the ear with a knife. In the struggle, Johnie cut his arm. Aunt Millipus and I ran up the stairs. You know that around here, colored people don't fight white folks.'

"'I see,' I said. 'Now, tell me something else? Did you know that Colonel George bought some land in Texas and willed it to Johnie, Jeannie Mae and Aunt Millipus?'

"He looked at me strangely and asked, 'How did you know that?'

"'Is it true Uncle Aaron?' I asked. 'Is it true that Col. George Jackson deeded some 200 acres of land to Aunt Millipus and her children?'

"'Yes ma'am, I did know that,' Uncle Aaron said. He continued, 'Colonel George left her some years ago and was gone some nearly two weeks. Then he called Aunt Millipus upstairs and told her he wanted to talk to her. I was in the other room and I heard him with these ears here. I heard him tell her about the land and that the deed was made out to her and her children. I heard him say he was going to put the deed in a leather bag in the trunk. If anything ever happened to her she would have a place to stay. I heard him say these words. He sometimes called her 'yellow breast.' He said he was giving her a key to open the trunk if anything ever happened to him. He would put a white string on the handle so that she would know which trunk it was. He told her that he wanted her to have everything in the black bag and that she was to have it if anything ever happened to him. Now that's what I heard with these two ears.'

"Uncle Aaron continued, 'After that, I eased out another door and neither Aunt Millipus nor Colonel George knew I heard the conversation. When Aunt Millipus left, that attic door was open the next day, and I went in there and found that little

137

trunk. There was not a black bag in that trunk with a string on it, so I surmised that she got that bag. I don't blame her. Then I locked the trunk.'

"I said to him, 'I want to thank you and your wife for this information. You are very kind.'

"'Lady,' she said, 'I'm glad to help, would you like a glass of water?'

"I said, 'Yes I would.'

"There was an oaken bucket with a dipper in the bucket. His wife got the water, and I drank it. Then I said, 'Tell me one more thing and I will be going.' I could tell the man in the hackney was getting restless.

"'If I can answer your question I will,' he said.

"'When Col. Jackson died, tell me what happened.' He said, 'Millipus and I were out there in the rose garden and we heard the shot. Millipus, she was just like a cat, could really run and jump. She outran me to the house. She beat me up the stairs, and I was pretty close behind her. But she got there first and opened the door and went in. She saw the gun still in his hand. She took it out of his hand and she was crying.' Uncle Aaron calmed himself. I asked, 'So you are saying that he was already dead when the two of you got there?'

"'Yes ma'am,' he said. 'He was as dead as a doorknob,' he said.

"I reached in my pocketbook and gave them some money which they tried to refused. But I insisted. Bidding them goodbye, I walked toward the gate. As I was about to open it, Uncle Aaron called me and said, 'Lady, you never told us about your real father. Is he still living?'

I said, 'In all truthness I don't know.'

'I see,' he said. He looked at his wife and it seemed there was a mental message going on between them. I said, 'I never knew him.'

"'Did Aunt Millipus know your father?' they asked.

"I answered, 'I suppose she did. But I never met the man. I don't know if he's dead or alive.'

Then Uncle Aaron's wife got up, and while accompanying me to the gate she took both of my hands and whispered softly to me something that I shall never forget. She said, 'Goodbye honey and may God bless you.'

"So I came back without any doubts in my mind that my grandmother, Millie Stone, had told the truth, and I swore that

138

when I came on this stand I would tell the whole truth and nothing but the truth and that's my testimony."

The judge replied, "If that's all Miss Webb you may step down."

She said, "There is one other thing. I found my uncle after I came back. I wrote to him, and he is present sitting over there with my parents. If you will look behind his ear, you will see a scar that he received in the fight trying to defend his sister. That is my Uncle Johnie."

The audience was surprised. She continued, "The man who has come here with all of these innuendoes and charges about my grandmother, that man who brought so much misery to my family, this man who came here contesting the will is, and I will repeat what Uncle Aaron's wife said to me that day at the fence."

Victoria said, "As she held my hand that day she said, 'My husband didn't want to tell you . . . he wanted me to tell you— Jeff Stanley is your father. When you walked off, you walked just like him. You have the same red hair, the same eyes . . . honey Jeff Stanley is your father. You are the very spit image of your papa Jeff Stanley.'"

Victoria said, " This man who has come here to destroy the principles of my grandmother—to taint her character—I am ashamed to say it, is really Jeff Stanley, my real blood father."

The courthouse was in a buzz and Jeff Stanley was on his feet crying, "My God, my God, I had no idea that I had a daughter. God please forgive me." He was almost crying.

Judge Griffin was pounding on his desk with the gavel for order. Jeff was still shouting, "My God, why didn't somebody tell me . . . why didn't somebody tell me."

Judge Griffin said, "Mr. Stanley, if you don't sit down, I will charge you with contempt of court. I mean sit down right now."

He sat down then and leaned over and put his face in his hands. Victoria said, "I'm going to ask the forgiveness of my parents who are dear to me . . . and of Trey, who to me is the greatest man on earth and whom I love dearly. To his grandparents who have already accepted me as their granddaughter—to all of my friends in the community and at the school who I know I have hurt. I am sorry that you had to go through this, but I could not live with myself had I not told you the truth. I told my parents last night. I told Trey, and I told his grandparents that I had made up my mind. I told them the truth and I told them I was going to tell it today. I know that this means good-bye to all of you. So I'll be leaving you and going somewhere else to pick up my life . . . maybe with my uncle and to really find out who I am. So I'm saying to all of you with a heavy heart—good-bye.

"I have one more thing to say. I went to visit my grandmother one week before she passed away. It was just about sundown and to my surprise she was already in bed. She said to me, 'Vickie, if you ever see your real papa, I want you to tell him something for me.'

"I quickly replied, 'I never want to see him,' to which she said, 'Honey, you can't keep hate in your heart. You have to pray and say, Let the will of the Lord be done. Tell Mr. Jeff Stanley that I said, 'at one time I hated his guts for what he did to me and my children, but I don't hate him anymore now. Even though it was hard, something good came of it, because he gave me you—my grandbaby, the only kinfolk in this world that I have as far as I know. This proves that God can bring some good out of a bad situation; because the people not only mistreated my Jesus they killed him. But on Sunday morning he got up from the grave and forty days later went on back to heaven.'

"Then she sat up in bed, clapped her hands and then extending her arms she shouted, 'Hallelujah, Thank you Lord. It won't be long now before he'll be coming back for me to take me to live with him in heaven forever more. Now you go home my child and let grandma rest.'

"I walked over to her and said, 'Goodnight, Grandmother, I love you.'

"I could not know that it would be the last time I would ever see her alive." Then looking straight at him, Victoria said, "Mr. Jeff Stanley I never thought I would live to see the day."

Turning to Judge Griffin she said, "Your honor, that is the end of my testimony." And with tears rolling down her cheeks she glanced toward her Uncle Johnie and his eyes were red because of tears he had shed during what to him was an agonizing testimony. Earlier that morning the two of them had gone to the cemetery and had laid a wreath on Aunt Millipus' grave. The bailiff escorted her from the witness stand.

As she stepped down Richard III got up from the seat where he was sitting with his grandparents. He walked up and met her and relieved the bailiff of her arm.

At that moment, Lawyer Glass stood up and said, "Your

honor, my client wishes to withdraw the lawsuit. He wishes the will to stand as read. Whatever the cost of court, we will pay it because we no longer wish to contest the will."

Judge Griffin said, "In that case then, I, as judge of this court, rule that the will is valid and will stand as read."

Richard III had pulled a handkerchief from his pocket and was wiping the cheeks of Victoria with one hand while holding her with the other. He kept saying to her that everything would be O.K. She said, "Please Richard, I've had enough."

He passed the seat where she had been seating. He kept saying, "It's going to be all right, it's going to be all right."

He ended up standing before the judge with her, and she wondered, "Is this the crucifixion? Is this the way that he is going to shame me before all of these people?"

He said to the judge, "Judge, Griffin I have in my pocket an envelope which has a marriage license that I purchased this morning for me and Victoria. I am asking you to marry us today. We had planned a big church wedding but after all of this, when we leave this courtroom I intend for Victoria to be my wife, and I want to take her home with me today. We love each other and I am determined to spend the rest of my life with her. If this means that I have to leave here and go to Kalamazoo, Michigan or to Buffalo, New York, that's what I'll do."

He took the envelope out of his pocket and extended it toward the judge. Somebody in the courtroom said, "He can't do that."

It was then that ole man Richard Koohne, who was leaning forward with both hands on his walking stick, stood up when he heard the person say that the judge couldn't do that.

The evening sunlight was shining on his partly bald red head, and his wife was sitting there beside him and seemed to have dressed for this occasion.

He looked back over the audience and asked harshly, "Who was that that said that?" There was a hush. Nobody said a word. Who in that courtroom or even that town could challenge this powerful old man. Not even the judge. He turned and faced Judge Griffin and said, "Marry them, Griffin."

He stomped the floor with his walking stick and stomped the floor again. "Marry them. By God marry them right now." And then as if he was talking to himself he repeated his favorite old adage, 'What difference will it make a hundred years from now?'

Judge Griffin opened the envelope that was in his hand, took the license out, and read them briefly. Victoria looked at Trey questioningly and said, "Trey you don't know what you're doing." Trey kept saying, "Honey it's going to be all right."

The judge reached and got a small book. He said, "Ladies and gentleman I hold in my hand a marriage license for Victoria Webb and Richard Koohne III. If there is anyone present who has reasons to believe that this couple should not be joined together in holy matrimony, speak now or forever after hold your peace."

Silence filled the room. He continued, "Who giveth this woman to this man?" Almost as if it had been a dress rehearsal, Walter Webb, her Uncle Johnie, and of all people, her father, Jeff Stanley all stood up. Johnie with his hand motioned to Walter Webb, and Jeff Stanley turned and motioned with his hand toward Walter. Walter Webb went forward and stood toward Victoria and said, "Judge Griffin, I do."

At that moment a few people on the aisle of the white side only got up and walked out. The judge went on with the ceremony. As they repeated their vows he asked for the ring. Richard pulled out a small box, opened it, and extended to the Judge a beautiful diamond wedding ring. He placed it on her finger, and the judge asked her if she had a ring. She replied, "No, I didn't know anything about this."

Trey said, "It's going to be all right."

At that moment Jeff Stanley stood up again interrupting the ceremony and pleading, "Judge, please I would like to give my ring to the bride as a wedding present to give to the groom—it is the least I can do to show my regrets for the terrible things that I've had this family go through because of my past actions and the suffering Aunt Millipus went through. Yet I guess I have mixed emotions. But I think I have to say this, I think I am the father of the most beautiful girl in Texas." He displayed a beautiful gold ring with a large blue diamond and turned to the bride and groom. He pleaded, "Please accept this gift as a tribute to the memory of your grandmother, whom I have come to know as one of the most courageous and noble women I have ever known."

Victoria looked at her parents with a question on her face and the father said, "Go on and accept it, baby—you have our consent." Then Jeff walked over to where she was and gave her the ring, clasping both hands and tenderly squeezing her hand,

and said, "This is from the bottom of my heart." She took the ring and handed it to the judge, and he took it and went on with the ceremony.

The judge went through the rest of the ceremony. He said, "I pronounce you man and wife. Richard you may salute the bride."

Richard took her gently in his arms and kissed her tenderly on her lips. The judge said, "Now you may face the audience." He said, "Ladies and gentlemen, I present to you Mr. and Mrs. Richard Koohne III."

There was some applause and some youngster in the rear said, "Show us the 'X'."

Jason stood up and pleaded, "Your honor Judge Griffin, please forgive me for interrupting the celebration, but I, too, have a presentation I would like to make before the audience disbands. May I have your permission?"

The judge looked around the room at the faces and seemed to have gotten the feeling that they were saying it was his decision. Jason took an envelope out of his coat pocket and addressed the town mayor, who had sat through the entire proceedings almost unnoticed by the people.

"Mayor McKnight, I have in this envelope a check I have written and signed that I would like to give to the town and community to purchase a fire wagon." He paused and after a moment continued, "I have ascertained the cost of the whole shebang, including the wagon, water tank, hose, pump, and two fast horses complete with bells. If you accept it, I would like it to be christened, 'The Khoonetown Community Aunt Millipus Memorial Fire Truck' in memory of Miss Emily Jackson. To me she is one of the most heroic negro women in these United States, second only to the late Mrs. Harriet Tubman. The check is on the Khoonetown First National Bank, of which you know Mr. Richard Khoone, Sr., is president. I am sure he will certify its validity."

Mayor McKnight stepped forward wearing his shining snakeskin boots and his expensive favorite buckskin jacket and received the envelope and extracted the check. After looking at it, he held it up to the audience and said, "People, it's all here, and it is something the town needs. If I say yes, we will accept it—do I express the sentiments of you all?"

A reply of yeses went around the room, followed by a round of applause. He then turned to Jason. "From the bottom of my heart, for all the people, thank you." Then he turned again to the people and blurted out the school yell they always did before the games started. He cried, "What's the matter with Angelina Khoone Town?" The answer came back from the audience, "She's all right." He repeated the question the second time and the answer came back louder, after which he asked, "Who said so?" The crowd answered, "Everybody." He questioned, "Who is everybody?" The answer resounded "Khoonetown, hooray!"

Mrs. Angelina Khoone, who had sat through the ceremony almost emotionless, was now smiling and was waving a beautiful silk handkerchief in approval of what turned out to be a grand occasion. Mayor McKnight went back to his seat, in a then-quieted audience, and as if almost talking to himself said, "What a day. Whoever would have thought I would have lived to see this happen in my time."

At that moment the chimes in the church began ringing and playing, "My country 'tis of thee." As Richard and Victoria marched down the aisle to the large doors that led to the streets, there were a few people on either side of the aisle joining in with the lyrics to the melody. "Land where my fathers died, land of the pilgrims' pride, from every mountain side let freedom ring."

Then from a remote corner of the courtroom came the distinct voice from a person who had gone unnoticed during the whole trial. The voice was that of Lazarus and he shouted, "Amen." He continued, "As Aunt Milipus always said, 'Let the will of the Lord be done.'" After a pause he said, "And ain't nobody mad but the devil."

About the Author

I was born on October 6, 1915, the third child of six. I grew up on a one-hundred-acre farm in the Brazos River Bottom Community, and completed the local black community school, Rock Dam Junior High, which had only nine grades. When the principal received permission from the state to add a tenth grade to the school system, I returned to school. At that time, all schools in Texas graduated students in only eleven grades. Since I still lacked one year to graduate, the principal searched for a scholarship at a small private college where I could get a high school diploma while also taking college courses. However, because of my mother's untimely death and my father's ill health, I was not able to attend college. At the age of seventeen, I assumed the responsibility of taking care of the family.

Although my father and uncle both owned the farm, it was on record as being owned solely by my uncle, who never had the records corrected to show the dual ownership. When my uncle passed away, the farm was claimed by his children, who, without telling anyone, sold the land. Fortunately, my mother had encouraged my father to purchase land in Marlin, Texas, and build a house on it just in case such a thing happened. Although he did purchase three lots and had built a house in Marlin, be-

145

cause of the economy there, we felt that we would be jobless, so my father arranged for us to move to a large farm, and we became sharecroppers to a white man named William D. Walker, who leased us 1,500 acres.

I worked for the Walkers for thirty-two years, and during that period our families grew into a close, almost kindred, relationship. Also during that time, a nice young lady moved into our community on a neighboring farm to take care of an aged and handicapped uncle. We struck up a relationship but could not even think of marriage because of our responsibilities. Our relationship ended shortly after the birth of our son, Lonnie, Jr., although we remain friends to this day.

My father died in February 1940, and that sort of disintegrated our family. In December of that year, another nice young lady moved into our community, and I got married and started a family of my own. We had four children, three boys and a girl—Cecil, Robert, Mike, and Norma. By that time I had become a foreman for the Walker family and was being paid a salary in addition to being able to farm some of the land.

I had always loved history and read everything I could get my hands on, including an old English book and an old Latin book. Being on a salary, I was furnished a pickup to do my chores, and I kept a newspaper, a magazine, a Bible, and murder mystery books in the seat, and at lunchtime I would read. I also talked with older people about history. During my time off, I visited libraries, cemeteries, and the courthouse.

I was reared in the local black church, called Cedar Grove Missionary Baptist Church, and always took a part in the activities. In my late twenties, I was elected president of the men's brotherhood association, which at the time had a membership of forty-seven churches. This projected me into the General Baptist Convention of the State of Texas, which at that time boasted a membership of 1,600 churches. In 1949 I was elected recording secretary of the brotherhood in the state and served in that capacity until I resigned in 1980. In 1992, in Tyler, Texas, I was honored man of the year in our state convention, and was able to attend national conventions in large cities from coast to coast, from the Gulf of Mexico to the Canadian border.

My family experienced a heartbreaking tragedy when at the age of eighteen our son Cecil suddenly died from what the doctors said was meningitis.

In 1966 the Walkers and I both retired from the farm, and I moved to Satin, into a house we had previously bought. I went to work for two years at a church furniture manufacturing company and then was employed by another company in the same city for thirty years before I retired, because of a losing battle with glaucoma. After doing rehab in the state facility for the blind in Austin, I was employed at the Light House for the Blind in Waco and eventually became shop foreman of the entire plant. I had gone to TSTC in Waco earlier to get my GED, and on the first writing part of the test, to my amazement, the instructor who graded my exam told me that according to the test I was among the ten percent of the smartest people in the U.S. (I had a problem with that.)

So after I retired from the Lighthouse for the Blind, I continued to be active in religious activities. I served as officer in the County Black Voters League, as an officer on the board in Waco EOAC, as the first black trustee on the Chilton ISD school board, an officer on two local Masonic Lodges, chairman of the deacon staff of our church and president of the local burial association, and song leader of the state brotherhood.

During those years I decided I wanted to write a novel to show that there was a relationship in the black and white generations, which would show the social climate and talk about the civil rights movement in the South. In 1999 I began writing my novel *Aunt Millipus and Her Will*, an historical fiction.

www.ingramcontent.com/pod-product-compliance
Lightning Source LLC
Chambersburg PA
CBHW051142020726
47501CB00005B/1643